WILMA RUDOLPH

Olympic Runner

Illustrated by Meryl Henderson

WILMA RUDOLPH

Olympic Runner

by Jo Harper

ALADDIN PAPERBACKS

New York London Toronto Sydney

To Josephine and
Lalo, with thanks

First Aladdin Paperbacks edition January 2004
Text copyright © 2004 by Jo Harper
Illustrations copyright © 2004 by Meryl Henderson

Aladdin Paperbacks
An imprint of Simon & Schuster Children's Publishing Division
1230 Avenue of the Americas, New York, NY 10020

Designed by Lisa Vega
The text of this book was set in Adobe Garamond.

Printed and bound in the United States of America
2 4 6 8 10 9 7 5 3 1

Library of Congress Control Number 2003107444
ISBN 0-689-85873-6

ILLUSTRATIONS

CONTENTS

Wilma Becomes a Fighter

Six-year-old Wilma waved sadly as her brother Wesley ran out the door. "See you later," he called over his shoulder. He was always going places and doing things—things he would joke and laugh about later. He was only a year older than Wilma and was her best pal. She wanted to go with him. Seeing him leave made her feel so lonesome she started to cry. It was the 1940s in Clarksville, Tennessee, and Wilma was stuck at home with only a little radio to listen to.

I don't get to go anywhere, she thought.

I'm tired of being left out. Everyone goes places except me. I always have to stay behind.

Wilma wasn't exaggerating. She didn't even get to go to school. She was too sick.

"Mother, why's my leg like this?" Wilma looked at the brace that was supposed to straighten her twisted foot and crooked leg. Then she looked intently at her mother's gentle face.

Mother answered kindly, but matter-of-factly. "You had polio. That's what twisted your leg."

"Why'd I get polio, Mother?"

"I reckon 'cause you were so weak. You were born early. I fell down, and you just came. You were so tiny and so sick, we were afraid you wouldn't live. You surprised a lot of people when you pulled through." She smiled. "You've always been full of surprises."

Wilma's brace was steel, and it went from her knee to her ankle. She couldn't take it off until she went to bed at night, and she always had to wear brown oxfords for the brace to fasten to. "I hate these shoes," she said. "Someday I'll buy myself a lot of fancy, bright-colored ones, and no one wearing brown oxfords can even come in my house."

Later Dr. Coleman came by to check on her. He was a black doctor, and he treated all the black people in Clarksville. He had taken care of Wilma all her life. He always wore a suit and carried his doctor's bag. Wilma thought he was very neat and very professional, but it was his face that she liked most. It was a kind, intelligent face. She always felt that Dr. Coleman understood her.

"I'm tired of being sick," Wilma told Dr. Coleman.

"I know, Wilma. I don't blame you," he said. "You've had a hard time. I've seen you fight scarlet fever, whooping cough, chicken pox, and measles."

"Don't forget pneumonia."

"I should say not! Double pneumonia twice! The last time, you were so weak everybody shook their heads over you, but you fought through that, too. You just keep right on fighting, little lady. If you fight hard, everything will turn out all right."

Wilma smiled in answer, but she felt lonely. *I don't have a single playmate outside my family. How can I make friends if I am always at home sick?*

Wilma didn't have nice clothes or toys; her family was too poor. They didn't have electricity or indoor plumbing. They used kerosene lamps and went to the bathroom in an outhouse. And because it was the 1940s and she was black, she didn't have equal rights as a citizen. What Wilma did have was plenty of brothers and sisters. In fact, Wilma had twenty-one brothers and sisters. She was child number twenty. And there were lots of aunts, uncles, and cousins. Her favorite aunt was Aunt Matilda. She often came to visit, and she would always play with Wilma.

Most of Wilma's brothers and sisters were grown and had moved out of the house, but five were still living at home. The grown ones came around often and helped Mother take care of Wilma. There were always people around, and it seemed to Wilma that some-one was always massaging her leg, but she was lonesome just the same. She wanted to be part of things. She wanted to do what other kids did instead of listening to the radio and daydreaming.

Wilma didn't even have to do household chores. Instead, she tagged after her brothers and sisters while they worked. She would go from one to the other, chatting with every-one, until all the chores were finished, and she never felt one bit guilty about not work-ing. She felt that talking to the others while they worked was her job. She kept them going; she was their cheerleader.

Wilma spent a lot of time looking out the

window. Often her mother sat with her. One day as they were sitting together, Wilma pointed to a boy walking by. "Mother, that's Robert, and he's the boy I like."

The boy was Robert Eldridge. He was lively and full of fun. When he realized that Wilma watched him as he went by her house, he began to show off for her to make her laugh. Sometimes he turned cartwheels; sometimes he brought a friend and played ball where she could see. He could hit the ball a long way, and he was good at catching.

The few times Wilma was well enough to go out to play with children her own age, they would tease her. Robert never called her names, but other kids called her "cripple." Her brothers and sisters stuck up for her, but it still wasn't much fun.

When she was at home sick, she wasn't happy either.

"Eat your supper, Wilma," Mother said.

"Not hungry." Wilma pushed her plate away.

"How can you get strong that way? I'll fix you a hot toddy."

Mother hurried to the stove and began putting together one of her famous home remedies. While the concoction boiled, she helped Wilma prop up in bed, and she piled lots of blankets on her.

"We're going to sweat that sickness out," Mother told her. She handed Wilma a glass. "Here's your hot toddy."

Wilma sipped it. It was almost boiling.

"Now, don't fool around. Drink it as fast as you can."

Wilma kept taking sips. She got hotter and hotter. Mother piled more blankets on her.

"Mother, I'm sweating to death."

"No, you're not. You are sweating to wellness. Drink all of that."

Wilma did. And believe it or not, she felt better.

But she couldn't fatten up by not eating and by sweating a lot. She stayed skinny. And while the brace may have helped straighten her leg, it injured her feelings. It reminded her every day that something was wrong with her. Especially in the spring and summer, when she woke in the morning with the sun shining and the birds singing, and she wanted to leap out of bed, run outside, jump off the porch, and play in the yard. Instead she had to put on her brown oxfords, put her twisted leg in the brace, and clunk through the house.

Having Wilma wear a brace wasn't the only attempt to straighten her leg. Twice a week her mother took her on a fifty-mile bus ride to Nashville. They went to a black hospital at Meharry Medical College.

"Maybe we can straighten that leg," Dr. Jackson told Mother. His face was serious, and he didn't include Wilma. He talked right past her, as if it were all up to Mother and Wilma didn't have anything to do with it. Dr. Jackson was a specialist and was supposed to know a lot, but Wilma preferred Dr. Coleman.

He never made her feel left out; he acted like she was in charge of her own life.

In the wintertime it was still dark when Mother awakened Wilma to go to Nashville. "Get up, Wilma. We have to get going." Mother spoke gently but firmly.

Wilma hated to get out of her warm bed. She limped into the kitchen to put her brace on by the fire. She had to move quickly; the bus wouldn't wait.

"Here. Eat this oatmeal. It'll warm you up."

"I can't, Mother. I'm not hungry."

"Eat anyway. You're never hungry, but you still have to eat."

So Wilma choked down a few bites of hot oatmeal before they left. Mother held her hand as they walked to the bus station. In her other hand, Mother carried their lunch bag, because there wasn't a café near the bus station that served black people. They took their places at the back of the bus, where black people had to sit. Wilma liked to look out the window. It was interesting to her to see the houses and farms they passed, and when they got to Nashville, she could see the city streets and the city people walking and driving their cars.

The hundred-mile round trip they made twice a week wasn't exactly fun. It was tiring, especially the ride home after a day of treatment, but Wilma felt like she was seeing the world. No one else ever seemed to leave Clarksville. Her brother Wesley was always going places, but he didn't get to leave town. Wilma was glad she had the chance to see more things, but it was a relief when, after two years of treatment, she and her mother started going only once a week.

At the hospital, the nurses kept pulling, turning, twisting, and lifting Wilma's leg. They strung it up with a little pressure on it. Wilma lay there with her leg up for an hour. They called that treatment "traction."

They are always pulling and twisting my leg, Wilma thought. *I don't know what good*

that's going to do. She didn't tell Mother that, though. Instead she lay patiently on a table with her leg in the air. The nurses read stories to Wilma as she lay there. All of them were nice to her, but her favorite was a large, older woman named Mary. She was calm and easygoing, and she acted as if she had all the time in the world to spend with Wilma. She had been a nurse for a long time, and she seemed to know a lot. She answered Wilma's questions about what was wrong with her.

"Mother said I have a twisted leg because I had polio," Wilma told her. "Do very many people get polio?"

"Yes, they do. I understand that there are about twenty-one thousand cases in the United States every year. That's more people than there are in the whole town of Clarksville."

"That's a lot, but I don't understand what polio is."

"It's a disease caused by poliovirus infection.

Sometimes people call it 'infantile paralysis.'"

"But that's just names. I want to know what is wrong with me."

"You were exposed to a virus—the poliovirus. All of us are, but our bodies fight it. Because you were weak, you couldn't fight it. It fastened on to some of your cells and then actually went into the cells."

I got polio because I didn't fight, Wilma thought. *I couldn't fight before—I was too little and weak. But I can fight now.*

"So, does everybody who gets polio have a crooked leg just like I do?"

"No. There are differences. If the infection is in the upper part of the spinal cord, it causes paralysis in the hands or arms. If the infection is in the neck part of the spinal cord, it affects the ability to breathe. But you were infected in the lower part of the cord. That causes weakness in the legs."

"Could somebody get sick from being around me?"

"Oh, no. Not anymore. You are over the infection, but it has left you with that weak leg. We are doing physical therapy to help your muscles get strong again. Right now it's time to take your leg down and massage it. Then you'll get in the whirlpool."

"I don't mind the massage, but I hate the whirlpool," Wilma told Mary.

She complained to Mother, too. "The water is too hot."

"Never mind. The key element is not the water; it's the heat. The heat will heal you."

So Wilma gritted her teeth and put up with the treatments.

It broke her heart to see how Mother watched her, hoping to see improvement. *I don't think all this stuff is doing any good,* she thought, *but I can't tell Mother that. I'm going to pretend I'm better so she'll feel good.*

Wilma fought hard not to limp. She tried to never give in to her weak muscles; she made them work even though it hurt her, and she got good at not limping.

I'm a fake. I can fake a normal walk, she thought.

Actually, she wasn't one bit of a fake. By making herself use the weak leg, she gave herself the best treatment of all. She strengthened her weak muscles.

Big Steps

Fighting loneliness and poor health, and struggling to walk without limping took a lot out of Wilma. It took so much out of her, she didn't feel like a real fighter at all. She felt like a scared little girl. When she was seven years old, she got to go to school at last. She went to the all-black school in Clarksville. It had grades kindergarten through twelve. She entered the second grade.

Wilma had spent so little time with children outside her family, she was terrified of them. She longed to have a friend her own age, but when she was near another child, she froze. She could hardly speak, and her stomach squeezed into a tight knot. More than anything, she wanted other children to like her, but she was sure they wouldn't.

"They won't like me," Wilma confided in her brother Wesley.

"Why not? I like you plenty." Wesley flashed her a grin. His teeth shone white in his handsome dark face.

"Yeah, but you're my brother. You don't care that I don't have pretty clothes or that my leg is twisted. They will."

On the first day of school Wilma stood at the edge of the playground at recess. She wanted to play with the other children, but she didn't know what to say or do. A girl named Nancy Bower came over to her. She had laughing eyes and a big smile. "Want to play jacks?"

Wilma was too shy to speak.

Nancy took her hand. "Come on. It will be fun."

Wilma followed her to where the girls were playing. "I don't know how," Wilma whispered.

"That's okay. I'll show you. It's easy." And it was easy. Wilma's hands were quick, and she had fun. But she was still scared.

They might not like me after they know me better. They'll get tired of seeing me in my brace.

Wilma was so afraid of not being accepted that she decided not to do or say any more than she had to. She thought she would be safe that way, but it was a nervous way to live. When she did have to speak, her voice was so soft people could hardly hear her, and she had to force herself to look up and meet their eyes. Sometimes she just couldn't do it. She was too scared. Her heart pounded and her face felt hot. She looked at the ground.

Wilma's first teacher, Mrs. Allison, seemed to understand, and she often asked Wilma to do special things for the class—things that wouldn't make her feel shy.

"Wilma, you are so artistic. Would you please decorate the bulletin board for me?"

Then Wilma would feel special. She could express herself by helping Mrs. Allison and not have to worry that she would lose the acceptance of the other students.

Mrs. Allison was also the leader of the Brownies. Wilma wanted to join, but her parents couldn't afford to buy her a Brownie uniform.

"That's all right," Mrs. Allison told her. "Just wear brown shoes or brown socks."

That Thanksgiving there was a parade downtown for the Brownies, and Wilma got to be in it. She stood as straight as she could and "faked" her walk. She could almost do it well enough to keep time with the band. Nancy Bower marched beside her. It felt wonderful to be marching with her friend in the group of Brownies. She was so proud, she held her head high. From the corner of her eye she could see Aunt Matilda and some of her brothers and sisters watching her march.

Now I'm just like everyone else, she thought. *I'm not sickly and left out anymore. I finally belong!*

Mrs. Allison did something else that was wonderful. She read stories to the class. Wilma loved to listen to her read. The stories opened up a new world. Wilma used her imagination when Mrs. Allison read, and it didn't seem like she was in the classroom at all. She was in the desert, or the jungle, or wherever the story was set. She didn't see her classmates or even Mrs. Allison. She saw the story. All the characters and their adventures were real to her. All her life, she remembered her wonderful first teacher and was grateful to her.

She was nine and a half years old when she finally was able to take off her brace. She was going to go to church. Everyone would see her. Everyone would notice. It was the biggest moment in her life. To be seen without her brace was exciting. But she was also worried. *What if I can't walk straight? What if I stumble?* She thought.

She put on her best dress and fussed with her hair. When she got to church, the congregation was already assembled. Wilma walked in, strode down the aisle, and took her seat. She was self-conscious, but she was proud. The members of the congregation applauded.

Taking off the brace didn't mean her treatments were over. She and her mother still went to Nashville once a week, and Mother kept making Wilma put a hot-water bottle on her leg. She could barely stand the heat, but Mother insisted that the heat would cure her.

The year she entered fourth grade, Wilma could hardly wait for school to begin. She didn't have to wear her brace, and she was sure that this would be the most wonderful year of her life. She spent a lot of time daydreaming about how dazzling she would be now, and what fun she would have. The teacher and the other students would love her, and she would do everything right.

But Wesley reminded her that the fourth-grade teacher was Mrs. Hoskins. She was a mean teacher. Everyone said so. No one wanted to be in her class. Wilma was scared, and it turned out she had reason to be. Mrs. Hoskins nagged Wilma all the time, and the tone of her voice showed that she meant business. If Wilma looked out the window, Mrs. Hoskins would speak sharply, "Stop daydreaming, Wilma! Pay attention!" Or, "Don't dawdle! Get busy!" It seemed to Wilma that she couldn't make a move without Mrs. Hoskins correcting her, and once she punished Wilma for not doing her homework.

"Wilma, come here."

Shocked and embarrassed, Wilma walked slowly to Mrs. Hoskins's desk.

"You know you were supposed to do your

arithmetic problems. Now stick out your hand."

Trembling, Wilma did. Mrs. Hoskins picked up a ruler and swatted Wilma across the hand—two sharp swats. The whole class was looking. Wilma was humiliated. She couldn't look up for the rest of the day.

If Wilma's father found out, he would give her a spanking. Although her parents had never spanked her, Father was strict about behaving well in school. He had told all his children that a spanking at school meant a worse one at home. Wilma was afraid of what Father would do. She was sure that Mrs. Hoskins would send a note home with her for her parents to sign. The note would explain how bad Wilma had been. But when school was over, Mrs. Hoskins didn't send a note.

Wilma felt sure then that Mrs. Hoskins would come by the house that evening to talk to her parents. She was so afraid, she couldn't eat a bite of supper or concentrate on the homework that she certainly had to get done. But the evening passed, and Mrs. Hoskins didn't come. She never told Wilma's parents. Wilma appreciated that, and although she hated to admit it, she knew that Mrs. Hoskins didn't play favorites. She treated everyone exactly the same, and she was very tough. But that was because she wanted everyone to learn; she expected a lot of all her students.

"Do it, don't daydream about it. Do it. Wilma, I want you to do it."

It took time, but Wilma came to love Mrs. Hoskins. She certainly never loved her fifth-grade teacher, though.

The fifth- and sixth-grade classes were together in one room. As an adult Wilma talked about how terrible the teacher was, but she didn't give his name. He was a big man; to Wilma he seemed like a giant, and his great wide face looked like an ogre's when he scowled.

He favored the sixth grade and ignored the

fifth graders. He played checkers with one student while the others were given class-work or had nothing at all to do. And he would give the students whippings across the hand for any little thing. He didn't give a quick swat with a ruler, as Mrs. Hoskins had. Instead he used a thick leather strap with a hole in it. He was a strong man, and he hit hard.

One day Wilma made mistakes in her class-work, and he told her to come to the front of the room.

He's going to hit me with that strap, Wilma thought. She didn't move from her chair. Her heart was pounding, but this time it pounded from anger as much as from fear. She felt he had no right to mistreat her.

"Wilma!"

She stayed put.

"Wilma! Come here!" She got up slowly and went to the front of the room.

"Hold out your hands."

Shy Wilma, who could usually only barely make her voice heard, spoke loudly and defiantly. "No, sir; you can't whip me for nothing. No, sir."

"Maybe you'd like to go see the principal, then."

"Yes, that will be fine."

The teacher was surprised. His big angry face looked shocked. He knew he was wrong and the principal would know it too. Wilma had called his bluff.

"Go back to your seat. The principal is too busy to talk to you today," he said. He never threatened her again.

Wilma had taken a big step. She had stood up for her rights. She had done what Dr. Coleman told her to do long ago. "Fight hard."

How Do You Fight Society?

Wilma had begun to learn to fight for her own rights, but she didn't know how to fight racism or discrimination. In fact, she didn't understand it, but she had to deal with it.

She was five when she first began to struggle with the idea that things were unfair. It happened when Clarksville was having the annual county fair. The black children got together and sat on the grass across from the main entrance. They braided the long grass as they watched white people going in and out. The white people were dressed in their best clothes, and they had beautiful horses. Wilma stared at them; they were a strange sight.

"Look at that lady's dress."

"Look at that man's fancy saddle."

"Yeah, and look at how they fuss over them horses."

Those folks live in a world I don't know anything about, Wilma thought.

At five years old she didn't understand prejudice, but she knew something was wrong. She began to tussle with the idea and to feel resentment. As she got older Wilma resented that her mother worked as a maid for rich white people. They had beautiful homes with every convenience, but her mother, who had no conveniences at all, served them breakfast in bed.

"It's not right that you have to do that kind of work," Wilma told her mother. "It's not fair. White folks get all the luxury, and we black folks get the dirty work."

"Never you mind," Mother said a little sharply.

"We have separate drinking fountains. Why? We can't eat in their restaurants. Why? We have to sit at the back of the bus and even give our seats to white folks. That's not fair."

Father raised his voice. "Shush up! Hold your tongue now!"

Mother and Father always told Wilma and her brothers and sisters that they had to accept things. They were trying to protect them, trying to keep them from getting in trouble. Most black families in the South were like that. But Wilma thought they shouldn't accept prejudice and injustice.

School didn't help her understand either. She wasn't taught anything about slavery or how things became the way they were. The school gave the students biographies of black people who had been successful. The trouble was that the school only emphasized that the students should be proud of them. It didn't look at what these people had to overcome. Like her family, the schools meant well. They thought they were protecting the children, but later Wilma said, "Keeping people ignorant isn't the way to protect them."

She personally met prejudice at a young age. She was at a white grocery store near her house. When the black children went there, they would keep very quiet, while the white children would giggle and act silly. Outside the store they did worse than giggle.

"Hey, nigger, get out of town!"

"Look out, darky."

"Enie, meanie, miny, moe, grab that nigger by the toe."

"Spook-spook-spook!"

"Teacher, teacher, don't hit me; hit that nigger behind that tree. . . ."

Wilma and her friends waited at the bottom of a hill, ready to fight. When they heard "nigger, nigger" again, they attacked. Fighting like that came to be a regular thing. The fights could be nasty, but Wilma got satisfaction out of them.

One thing that caused her to notice prejudice was her own color. Her skin was light and her hair was a sandy red. Her brother Wesley had dark black skin. Wilma's brothers and sisters were all different colors. That was because her mother was jet black, but her father had a pale complexion.

People sometimes thought Wilma was white, and when she was out with Wesley, she would hear comments like, "Hey, little girl, why are you walking with *him*?" That happened more than once, and it made Wilma feel strange. She told her sister Yvonne how she felt.

"Color shouldn't make so much difference."

"It shouldn't, but it does," Yvonne answered, giving her a hug.

And because of her bad experiences, color began to make a lot of difference to Wilma, too. She began to think white people were wicked people.

Hope and Disappointment

The summer before Wilma entered seventh grade, she discovered basketball. She was strong enough now that she could go to the parks in Clarksville where black children played. The parks were just little squares of grass with a few shrubs. There wasn't any playground equipment, but in some of them there was a pole. In order to play basketball, the kids would cut the bottoms out of baskets to make hoops and attach them to the poles. They played in their backyards, too, and by now Wilma had made many friends.

They didn't care if all they could find was a tennis ball. They would shoot it into the homemade hoop anyway.

Wilma fell in love with the game of basketball. It was fast, and you had to concentrate, which she liked. But what she liked best was that she didn't have to run to play. She could just stay in one place and wait for her shots.

"I'm too clumsy to run," she told Wesley, "but I can learn to shoot from one spot."

"Yeah. If you work at it, you'll get to be a good shooter that way. But don't stand still; keep moving around in place."

Because Wilma had been sick so much, her mother was very protective. She didn't want Wilma to tire herself out. "You take it easy, now," she said as she left for work.

"Yes, ma'am," Wilma answered. But she didn't take it easy. She played basketball.

When her mother came home, she asked, "What did you do today?"

Wilma answered truthfully. "I played basket-ball all afternoon."

"What? Didn't I tell you to take it easy? What were you thinking of? You know better than that. You'll make yourself sick."

"But, Mother . . ."

"Not another word. I don't want you play-ing basketball, and that's final." Mother went to the kitchen with an angry face.

When Mother was gone, Wilma went to Father and asked, "Can I go out and play basketball?"

"Sure. Why not?" Away she went, and played for hours. This happened several times.

Of course, Mother found out. "What you're doing isn't nice—getting your father's permis-sion to play basketball after I already told you no." Mother and Father didn't normally spank Wilma, but this time Mother got a switch and whipped her hard. It was terrible, but hearing her father and mother quarreling later was worse. Mother was mad because Father had let her play, and Father was mad because Mother had given her a spanking.

Hearing them quarrel was so painful, Wilma stopped being sneaky. But she didn't have to give up basketball for long, because school started, and Mother didn't object to her playing for the school.

Clarksville had a brand-new black school— Burt High School. The seventh through twelfth grades went there. And Burt High School had a girls' basketball team. All grades could try out for it.

Wilma told her father that she wanted to play on the team. Her father believed strongly in family togetherness. He told Wilma's older sister, "Yvonne, you take Wilma along with you to play basketball, you understand?"

Yvonne didn't complain that Wilma was too young or that she would be trouble. She was a loyal sister, and she introduced Wilma to Coach Clinton Gray. "My sister Wilma is a great shot, and she wants to join the team."

Coach Gray let her join. Yvonne was a good player, and he wanted to keep her. Maybe he knew how Wilma's father felt about togetherness; if Wilma couldn't be on the team, neither could Yvonne. So he let a skinny little seventh-grade girl with a weak leg on to the team. For once, Wilma was glad Father was so strong in his opinions.

I can play just like the big girls, she thought excitedly. *Now that I'm on the team, I can play against other schools. I'll get to play on a lot of basketball courts.*

But Wilma didn't get to play a single game. She sat on the bench the whole season. That was hard to take.

It's just because I'm so young, she told herself. *Other seventh graders aren't playing either.*

Wilma didn't waste her time while she was on the bench. She studied everything that was happening on the court. She learned all the rules of the game; she learned how the rebounders position themselves; she learned how to make people foul you when you are shooting, so you will get two free throws.

Wilma got to travel, too. The team went to other towns in Tennessee and to Hopkinsville, Kentucky. On long trips the team had to sleep on the bus. When Wilma got home at five in the morning, Mother was up fixing breakfast.

"Mercy me, child. That basketball is going to kill you. You get right to bed; you don't need to go to school today."

"Oh, I don't want to miss school. I'll just rest a little while."

"Sleep until noon, then. If those teachers are going to keep you up all night, they can't expect you to be at school in the morning."

But Wilma was in her place when the tardy bell rang. So were the other team members. School was the center of their social lives, and staying home was a bore.

Basketball is something I can really do

well, Wilma thought. *I can do it as well as anybody. Better. Maybe I can be a star. Maybe I can be a school hero.*

That was her dream; it was a dream she could work to make come true, but it was also the kind of dream that didn't fit the attitudes of Clarksville, Tennessee.

"Girls aren't athletes," Mother's friend Mrs. Simpson told Wilma. "Or at least, they shouldn't be." She folded her hands in her lap and stretched her neck long, like she was very proper and elegant.

"She's right," another friend, Mrs. Walter, said, touching her hair. "It's not ladylike. You'll develop muscles like a man. Then who'll marry you?"

Wilma hated that kind of thinking. She bit her tongue. She had been taught to be respectful of older people, but it was hard for her not to argue.

"Yes'm," she said. She had to look down when she said that, and she excused herself as soon as she could. She knew her mother's friends were wrong. She wouldn't listen to them.

I love sports, but I'm a lady, she thought. *Nobody likes pretty clothes and dressing up more than I do. And just look how I managed not to answer back to Mother's friends. That was very ladylike; Mother taught me good manners.*

Wilma kept her dream. She saw herself dribbling the ball and maneuvering across the court. She saw herself leaping high and making a basket. She saw herself winning free shots and making the basket on every one. In her mind the crowd applauded and shouted her name, "Wilma! Wilma!" She had big dreams, but she dreamed from the bench.

It had been a long time since she'd needed to stay in one place to play. Her sister Yvonne commented, "I remember when you had to stand in one place. Now you are all over the court. You are quick as a whip!"

Wilma knew that was true. At practice she tried to catch Coach Gray's eye. She wanted him to see how quick she was now and how well she could shoot. But he hardly noticed her.

Wilma hoped that when she was in the eighth grade she would get to play. It made sense that Coach Gray picked older players. But as an eighth grader, she'd be older. She even mentioned it to Coach Gray's good friend Mrs. Mildred Jones, another teacher. She thought Mrs. Jones might put in a good word for her, but Mrs. Jones said, "I expect you do have a better chance as an eighth grader, but I wouldn't dream of mentioning it to Coach Gray. That would be interfering. Just do your best."

Wilma practiced hard all through the summer. Eighth grade would be different. She would play every game. She would wow the crowd.

But that wasn't how it turned out. Again she spent almost the whole season on the bench. Until one game when their team was far behind and there were only a few seconds left, and Coach Gray called her onto the court.

It was her first chance and instead of making a good showing, she panicked. In the few seconds she was on the court, she stumbled and dropped the ball. That didn't make the coach think better of her, and she was furious at herself.

She got another chance at a game when the team was winning by so many points they couldn't lose. There were only a few seconds left in the game and Coach Gray sent Wilma in.

Somebody threw her the ball. She caught it—a solid catch. The ball felt comfortable in her hands. "Shoot! Shoot! Shoot!" the crowd yelled. The people were only a blur to her. She focused on the hoop.

Coolly, Wilma made a one-handed push shot. In it went! She could hardly believe she had made a basket. It was a remarkable shot.

When the basketball season ended, Coach Gray announced, "I think I'll start a girls' track team. Would any of you girls like to go out for track?"

Wilma didn't hesitate even one moment. "I would." Being on the track team would give her something to do after school.

The coach started them out jogging. Just jogging. That was fun for Wilma. In a few days he divided the team into groups of six or seven. He stood in the middle of the field and said, "Run past me as fast as you can."

The groups ran past him, one after the other. The first time Wilma ran, she started slowly, but she picked up speed halfway to the coach and beat everyone else. She didn't think much about it, though. Track was just for fun. Basketball was serious competition.

By the ninth grade Wilma was really dying to play basketball. She had spent two years on the bench and two summers practicing. She had studied the way people dribble and the way they move. She could tell whether they were concentrating or not. She learned to steal the ball, and she was good at it.

She realized that when you steal the ball, it does more than give it to your team. It gives you an emotional advantage. Having a ball stolen in front of everyone makes a player feel bad, which makes it harder for that player to do well.

Wilma thought for sure she would get to play that season because she had become so good at stealing the ball. But the coach still didn't seem to know she was alive. To Wilma that didn't make sense; she knew she was a good player.

Finally Wilma got mad. "Coach Gray, how come I'm not playing?"

He ignored her.

Wilma got madder. "Coach Gray, I want you to know that if you gave me as much time as you give some of the other girls, I'd be a star."

Coach Gray laughed. "Okay," he said. "Come

to practice tomorrow ready to play hard."

Wilma did. She came with high hopes, thinking things would change, but they didn't. She sat on the bench another year. That made three straight years of biding her time.

"I'm going to go out for track again," she told Wesley at the end of the season.

"Might as well," Wesley said, "but Coach Gray's not a serious track coach. He just has track to keep the basketball players in shape."

"I know, but it's fun. I like to run."

The truth was, the girl who once could hardly walk now loved to run. She loved the fresh air. She loved the feeling of freedom. And somehow, she felt that she was really just competing against herself. She wasn't thinking about the other girls; she was just trying to do better than she had before. She liked that.

Wilma ran in five different events that year, the relay and the 50-, 75-, 100-, and 200-meter races. One event was in Columbia, Tennessee. The school there didn't have a running track.

They just had a field. They had set up lanes, but they were hard to see, and the players drifted out of their spots. Wilma lined up for the 200. The flag dropped, and they were off . . . but Wilma stepped on a big rock. It hurt, and she lost her pacing. She kept going. Then she stepped into a hole.

"Ouch! My ankle!" It was nearly broken, but she kept running. She raced straight ahead. *Where is the finish line? It drives me crazy not to know where I am,* she thought. *I can't do it right if I don't know how far I have to go.*

Wilma won the race, but she told her coach, "I don't want to run the two hundred anymore."

"Why not?"

"I can't stand not knowing where the race ends."

Wilma did run it again, though, many times. She won twenty races that spring, but she still didn't take running seriously. She had her heart set on playing basketball.

"I'm nearly six feet tall," she told Wesley. She could look him squarely in the eyes now. He was only a little taller than she was.

"I know it, Long Legs," he said, sinking down on their front step. "You're the stringiest string bean I ever saw."

"Look at my arms. They're long too. Real long." She stretched her creamy arms above her head and stood on tiptoe.

Wesley looked amused. His eyes twinkled in his dark face. "So what, Giraffe?"

"Maybe I can be center on the basketball team next year."

"For Pete's sake, Wilma, basketball is all you ever think about. Don't you know what you are good at? You are a runner!"

Wilma gave that some thought. It seemed a little funny to her. She had started playing basketball because she didn't have to run. Now it seemed that she was better at running than at basketball.

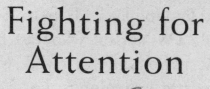

Fighting for Attention

Wilma was five-feet-eleven and weighed eighty-nine pounds. That was eighty-nine pounds of sheer determination. She was determined that as a tenth grader, she would really play basketball, so she made a two-part plan. The first part was to get in tip-top shape. The second was to get Coach Gray to take her seriously.

Wilma's best friend, Nancy Bower, was her ally. Before school started, they made a habit of going to the basketball court at the school playground. They would persuade anyone they could find to play with them. Even their friend Delma Wilkerson, who wasn't the least bit athletic, played once in a while when they were desperate. Sometimes they were lucky and got to play with members of the boys' basketball team. When that happened the girls had a good challenge.

The second part of Wilma's plan was harder. How could they make Coach Gray really notice them? Wilma thought about it night and day.

Coach Gray was in charge of a special performance every year. Mrs. Jones helped some, but it was really Coach Gray's project, and it required a lot of his time and attention. It was a minstrel show with tap dancing and singing. The students in the show practiced at one end of the gym. Wilma thought this offered the chance she and Nancy wanted.

"Coach Gray, since the gym is being used anyway, is it all right if we come and shoot some baskets?"

The answer was no.

Wilma and Nancy weren't prepared to accept that answer, but they knew better than to argue. Instead they worked out a strategy. They would get Coach Gray in a really happy mood and then ask again.

The way to get him in a happy mood was to get him talking about the good old days. It took only a couple of leading questions to get him started. He was full of stories, and he laughed and told one after another. Then, at just the right moment, Wilma slipped the question to him.

"Can we come in and shoot?"

The very next day they went to the gym to shoot. They took two boys from the boys' team with them, and they started dribbling and shooting—having fun. Suddenly Coach Gray came up and told them to get out of the gym. He said the sound of the dribbling interfered with the minstrel show practice. But Wilma wasn't about to give up. She went to him later and spoke seriously. "Coach Gray, basketball means more to me and Nancy than anything else. We want to be great players, so we have to practice every chance we get."

Wilma's honest appeal worked. "Okay, I'll put up with the dribbling. Just keep the noise down."

Every afternoon Wilma and Nancy practiced from three fifteen until five. Coach Gray couldn't keep from noticing them. Wilma hoped they made an impression. They wanted to be starters—the team members who play at the beginning of a game.

Coach Gray was very secretive. Wilma and Nancy studied his expressions and hung on his every word, trying to figure out who would get to start, but they didn't have a clue. Coach Gray never gave the least sign of who he would pick. The suspense was killing them. When would he tell them? The night of the first game rolled around, and he still hadn't said a single word about starting.

The girls went to the locker room and dressed in their uniforms. "We're the best," Wilma whispered to Nancy. "Coach Gray knows that."

"Maybe he doesn't," Nancy whispered back. "Maybe he doesn't think we're so hot."

They all went out onto the floor to warm up. Finally the buzzer sounded. They went back to the bench. How much longer would he make them wait? It was nearly time for the game to begin.

Coach Gray walked across the gym toward the girls. There was no expression on his face that gave any sign of who he might choose. Then he started down the bench. He pulled the sleeves of the girls he wanted to start. Wilma stared hard as he pulled one girl's sleeve, then another's. She couldn't sit on the bench again. She just could not. And she knew she should not. She deserved to start the game. He must know it too. Was he trying to torture her? He pulled Nancy's sleeve.

Then he pulled Wilma's. She heaved a sigh. She had made it. She would play guard and forward.

That was a victory for Wilma, but it didn't mean the season was smooth sailing. Coach Gray often yelled at the girls. He even did it during games when all the people who came to watch could see and hear. He yelled at Wilma just as much as at any other girl, but Wilma wasn't just any girl. She wouldn't take that kind of treatment.

One night he shouted at her during a game. The next day at practice she confronted him. "Don't you yell at me in front of everybody!" she told him.

"Play right and I won't have to yell!"

"I quit!" Wilma stalked off the court and went home.

She stayed away for a whole day—until the next practice. She just had to play, no matter what. Besides, even if Coach Gray did shout at the girls, Wilma came to realize he just did it because he was so involved with them and their games. He was a dedicated coach, and he really cared about his players.

Coach Gray made them keep their grade averages at least a B. He also insisted that they be dressed and on the practice floor by three thirty every day. No questions, no excuses. He was a football coach too. During football season he would show up at basketball practice wearing his football pants and his cleats. He would get the girls started, then go back to football practice. After the basketball practice he would take each of the girls home in his little Valiant. He did all that for only about two hundred dollars a year extra pay; that's how dedicated he was. So Wilma put up with his outbursts and looked for a way to earn respect.

One way she could earn respect was by helping the team win. That year the team won all eleven of their conference games. That meant they won the Middle East

Tennessee Conference title. Wilma felt that her part in their victories was a big step toward winning respect.

The conference games were actually supposed to be the important games because they were against other good teams and could lead to a state championship, but to Wilma, the most important game was a little tournament that was played just for fun and couldn't win state recognition. It was played during school hours so all the students could watch. Most of the time, her schoolmates didn't get to see the games. They couldn't afford the price of admission. But they were all at the free tournament. People Wilma knew filled the gym. She cared what they thought, and she wanted to impress them. Since she cared so much, she was nervous about playing badly. Even now, she worried about being accepted and keeping people's approval, so she tried hard, and she did better than make a good showing. She scored thirty-two points; she didn't miss a single shot or a single free throw.

"How did you do that?" someone asked her.

"Long legs and determination!"

Now Wilma was not only accepted, she was a school hero—just as she'd always dreamed she would be.

Learning to Lose

Because the girls' basketball team won the conference title, they had a spot in the state tournament—the Tennessee High School Girls' Championships of 1956. They were held at Pearl High School in Nashville, Tennessee.

Coach Gray made wonderful arrangements for the team—they stayed with his sister who lived in Nashville. She was married to a university professor and had a nice house. She was Coach Gray's favorite sister, and she loved having the girls stay with her. That made things special for them. Her name was Phyllis, and the girls called her Miss P. The *P* could have stood for "patient." She laughed and joked, and nothing seemed to upset or bother her. She and Coach Gray were both tall, and their round faces looked alike, but that's where the resemblance ended. He was as intense as his sister was easygoing. Everything mattered to Coach Gray; he took everything seriously. He lived in extremes. He was on top of the world or down in the dumps. He expressed everything he felt loudly and often, and when it came to basketball, his temper was terrible. He could be a frightening man.

Wilma met another very interesting man on this trip. He was the referee for the games, Ed Temple. He was tall and athletic like Coach Gray, but the two men were totally different in every other way. Coach Ed Temple had a square, handsome face and a quiet, dignified manner. He didn't seem to want to share all his thoughts and feelings. He made Wilma think of an expression her mother used: still water runs deep. Wilma liked Coach Temple. He was fair, and instead of calling her a number, he called her "Rudolph." With the help of Coach Gray, Coach Temple came to be a powerful influence on Wilma.

Once he came over to Wilma and said, "Rudolph, you're too lazy to jump." Then he put a mark on the wall and spoke to Coach Gray. "Rudolph should jump at this mark twenty or thirty times a day until she can hit it."

"Good idea," Coach Gray answered. "I'll see that she does that."

"When she can hit it, move the target up and have her start over."

Wilma was fifteen years old and in the tenth grade. That was young to be playing in the state tournament, but she scored twenty-six points in the first game, and her friend

Nancy, scored thirty. The Clarksville team won. Wilma and Nancy congratulated each other. "We are going to win the whole thing!"

"We'll go down in history as a Cinderella team!" Wilma believed her own words. *We are the best*, she thought. *The youngest and the best. This is too easy; it's a cake walk.*

But they made a lot of careless mistakes and lost the second game by eight points. The team was cut from the tournament.

"We're not Cinderellas," Nancy said.

"We're sure not. We're pumpkins." Wilma tried to joke, but she was crying. She and Nancy were too disappointed to watch the rest of the games.

How could I have played so badly? Wilma thought. *I don't want to see anyone. It is too embarrassing. I can't stand to look Coach Gray in the eye. I've let him down. He probably hates me now.*

Coach Gray didn't act like he hated her. He worked her hard, though, and he did make her jump at least twenty times every day. The target line went up and up. As soon as basketball season was over, Wilma was ready to run, but she kept jumping just as Coach Temple and Coach Gray said she should.

Wilma had a friend named "Sundown." His real name was Edward, but everybody called him Sundown because he was so black. Wilma and Sundown started cutting classes together and sneaking across the street to the city stadium where there was a good track and the teachers couldn't see them. They'd throw their books over the wall, climb the fence, and run on the track there. They were always in danger of getting caught. If they did, they'd be in big trouble.

A few times when they climbed over the wall, they found the place full of white runners practicing. They were from Austin Peay College. They noticed Wilma and Sundown but didn't say anything, just went on with

their practice. The coach gave Wilma and Sundown an expressive wink. It showed that he knew what was going on, and that he had a little admiration for their dedication. When that coach talked to his team, Wilma would listen from a distance. He was a college track coach, and she knew he knew a lot about running. He noticed her trying to overhear and started talking louder.

One day the principal called Wilma to his office.

"Wilma, we all know how important running track is to you. We hope you will become a big success. But you can't keep cutting classes to run."

Wilma stood there, embarrassed and silent.

"In fact, Wilma, if you cut any more classes, I'll have to tell your father."

She knew she would be in big trouble if Father found out. He was strict and wouldn't put up with any foolishness. He might even stop her from playing sports. So Wilma quit cutting class. But she was the first one at practice every day, and the last one to leave. She really loved to run, and she kept winning every race she was in. She felt unbeatable.

The biggest track meet of the year was in Tuskegee, Alabama. Girls from all over the South came. They stayed the whole weekend, and there were dances and other social events for them as well as the track events.

On the way down Coach Gray told them that the competition was tough. The girls from Atlanta, Georgia, were formidable. There were a lot of black schools there, so there were a lot of runners to choose from, and the weather was warmer than in Tennessee. In Atlanta the girls ran all year long.

Wilma wasn't worried. She knew she could wipe them out. Hadn't she won every race that year? But Wilma got wiped out herself. She didn't win a single race, and she didn't qualify for anything. She was crushed.

Wilma still couldn't take losing in stride, and she was so upset, she wouldn't go to any of the activities—not even the big dance.

Wilma had been overconfident again. Winning so many races had given her the feeling that she was unbeatable. She found out that she wasn't. She also found out that natural ability alone wasn't enough. Those Georgia girls had been trained in running techniques, and they knew every trick in the book. Wilma didn't know any techniques or any tricks. Her confidence was shattered, but she was determined not to be beaten down by losing those races.

All day, every day, Wilma thought about running, and she ran every day—long runs— except on days when she was too depressed. Then she moped around and felt sorry for herself. Sometimes she had fire in her eyes, sometimes tears.

Wilma realized she was being tested. Would the defeat stop her as a runner? Was she too crushed to fight on? Or did she have it in her to make a comeback, to be victorious?

Finally Wilma understood that she had to change her attitude. She had to learn to lose. Anyone who wanted to be a champion had to learn that lesson.

Wilma won the rest of the races that season, but she was sure anyone who saw her lose so badly in Tuskegee would never think she had the makings of a champion. She was dead wrong. The referee, dignified Coach Ed Temple, who was also the head coach of women's track and field at Tennessee State College, came to Clarksville to talk with her parents. He had given his team the name "Tigerbelles," and he had made them into champions. He could spot talent, and he knew Wilma had it. He asked her parents if she could spend the summer at Tennessee State, learning running techniques.

Father was an old-fashioned man, a strict, proud one. As poor as they were, he wouldn't accept "relief," which is what they called welfare in those days. He was too proud to take money he hadn't earned. And he laid down the law to his children: They had to go to church. "No church on Sunday morning, no anything else." Whenever Father came home, everyone got quiet.

Father was illiterate, but that didn't keep him from making all the decisions in the family. If something needed to be read, Wilma's mother read it out loud to him, and then he made the decision. Whether or not Wilma got to go to Tennessee State was up to Father, and he was protective of his fifteen-year-old daughter.

Wilma was afraid he wouldn't let her go for the summer to work with Coach Ed Temple. As always when she was nervous, her stomach tied itself in knots. She knew that she really needed Coach Temple's instruction. Seeing how the Georgia girls ran had made her realize that she couldn't be a first-rate runner without help. But Father wouldn't understand that; he probably didn't think it mattered if she learned to run better or not. She wanted to beg him, but she was afraid if she said too much it would be worse than if she kept quiet and left the persuading to Coach Temple. She knew he was a man who inspired confidence.

Mother and Father listened to what Coach Temple had to say. They were cordial, but Wilma knew that didn't mean they'd let her go.

"Mr. Rudolph, the summer track program is for high school runners who show promise to be outstanding athletes. Wilma shows great promise. This is an opportunity for her to really develop her talent." Coach Temple's quiet voice carried authority.

Father listened politely. His expression didn't change. Wilma's heart beat faster.

"If you decide to let her participate in the program, she will be safe and well cared for. Mrs. Perkins, a track coach from Atlanta, lives in the dormitory with the girls. She is on the same floor with them and watches over them carefully. And during the day, Pappy Marshall, our equipment manager, helps. He is a kind, responsible man, and he looks after the girls like a second father."

The expression on Mother's face made Wilma think she might be in favor of letting her go, but Father would make the decision, and his expression hadn't changed one bit.

"Wilma's expenses will be paid by the college. She won't need any money except spending money. Of course, if she should go home for the weekend, she would need bus fare, but that's all."

Father didn't say a word.

"Maybe you would feel better about it if you read the rules." Coach Temple handed Father a sheet of paper. He didn't know that Father couldn't read.

"Let me read it to you," Wilma said. "I have young eyes." She read:

"Girls must be in their rooms by nine
   o'clock every night.
Girls' lights must be out by ten o'clock
   every night.
Girls must be up by seven o'clock in the
morning.
Girls are forbidden to ride in cars.
Girls are forbidden to go to nightclubs.
Girls must attend church on Sunday
   mornings."

Father thought Wilma was too young, but
he was reassured about her safety and about
quiet, dignified Ed Temple's character. He
considered carefully, and finally he agreed.

Wilma was about to have the most important summer of her life.

Running Right

Coach Temple took it on himself to drive to Clarksville to get Wilma. On the road, they didn't even talk about track. They talked about their common love: basketball.

When they arrived at Tennessee State College, Wilma went to a dormitory called "Wilson Hall." College girls were living there. Soon other high school girls who were going to be part of the track training session began to arrive. Wilma was the youngest, but she made friends easily. One of her good friends was Shirley Crowder. Shirley was a good pal, a talented athlete, and an elegant dresser. Wilma thought that if her mother's friends who had said playing sports wasn't ladylike could see Shirley, they'd surely change their minds.

The girls' training was intense. They ran every morning from six until eight. They would then have breakfast and rest until ten thirty. Then they would run six miles, have lunch, and rest. At three in the afternoon they would run another six miles.

All the running was cross-country, through farmland and over hills. Wilma learned to breathe freely and easily, and all the girls built their endurance.

Then they were ready to learn techniques.

One simple technique was valuable to Wilma—keeping the fists loose. She learned that the less tense your muscles are, the better you can run, and that if you run with clenched fists, your other muscles tighten too. If you run with open hands, your whole body tends to be loose. Another simple technique was leaning into the race, not away from it. Coach Temple worked with them on these techniques. He also worked so hard on building group spirit that the girls really became a team, not a bunch of individuals. Surprisingly that made for intense competition, but it was competition between friends.

Wilma discovered that each runner is different and has a different set of problems. She had two. One was: She had trouble coming out of the starting blocks. That meant it took her a while to build her speed. It took her about forty-five feet just to get going, so she was better at the long runs than the short ones. Even though she was slow in starting, she was great at overtaking the other runners. The other problem was: Wilma couldn't relax before a race. She would get a terrible feeling in the pit of her stomach, and sometimes she would even vomit.

Coach Temple put Wilma on the relay

team. To be effective on a relay team, a runner has to know the other members very well—their reflexes, their timing, their reactions, their moves—and of course, must also know the relay routine perfectly.

In a relay race the runner must pass the baton to the next runner, who then runs and passes it to the next runner, and so on. Passing the baton is not easy. It is the passer's job to get it into the receiver's hand. The passer can see both the baton and the receiver's hand, but the receiver can't see either. She has to look straight ahead. The receiver starts running as soon as she feels the baton. The handoff is hard for the passer because she is running fast, but if she doesn't do it right, the receiver will start with a handicap.

Coach Temple took the girls all the way to Philadelphia to the National Amateur Athletic Union meet. Wilma sat in the front seat beside him, since her legs were too long to fit in the back. When he took her to Franklin

Field, she was surprised to see how big it was. She had never seen a stadium that big. It made her feel uneasy.

She ran in it, though—the 75, the 100, and the 4 x 100-meter relay. Wilma ran in nine races and won them all, but nobody paid any attention to her victories. Even Coach Temple remained very reserved. He quietly complimented her, but he didn't show excitement. Just the same, Wilma's confidence was back strong. She had fought back from the defeat at Tuskegee.

Getting to meet Jackie Robinson didn't hurt her confidence either. One of the meet directors asked Coach Temple to bring a couple of girls to get their pictures taken with him. Wilma was chosen.

Jackie Robinson was the first black man to play major league baseball. He was a hero to black athletes and to all black people, and he was admired by whites, too. Born in 1919, he was twenty-one years older than Wilma and had already made history as an athlete and as a person who advanced the rights of black people. Robinson had to endure racial remarks from the other players as well as the fans, but he proved himself as a person and as an athlete. He quit baseball in 1956, the year Wilma met him, in order to devote himself to political and civil rights work.

Jackie Robinson was a role model in more ways than one, and he took an interest in Wilma. She was shy, and she never expected to have to talk, but he asked her where she was from and how long she had been running. He was surprised to learn that she was still in high school. "You are a fascinating runner and don't let anything or anybody keep you from running. Keep running."

Wilma had met her first real black sports hero, and he had praised her. She cherished his advice.

Skeeter Baby

"I'm taking a bunch of my college girls up to Seattle, Washington, for the Olympic trials, and I want you to come with us."

"Wow! Okay, Coach Temple." Wilma was surprised that he was inviting her to go run with experienced college athletes and to make a long trip from Tennessee to Washington state. That was exciting. But Wilma didn't realize just how exciting the invitation was. She had no idea what the Olympics were. She didn't know that all the countries in the world competed in the Olympic Games, or that it was a tremendous honor to be selected for the Olympic team. Those were things she would find out later.

Wilma was amazed that she, a sixteen-year-old high school girl, had a chance to be a part of the Olympics. She felt overwhelmed and shy. Maybe Coach Temple knew she would react that way, and that's why he didn't explain how important the Olympics were. He was very casual about the whole thing. Wilma got most of her information from the other girls who were going to compete. She made friends with them on the long ride to Seattle.

Her most important friend was Mae Faggs. Mae was only four-feet-ten-inches tall, but little Mae was a big star. She had set all sorts of U.S. records in women's track, and she had won medals in the Olympics. The other girls looked down at her physically but looked up to her as an athlete and as a person. As a sportswoman Mae was a great competitor; as a friend she was generous and tactful.

Coach Gray gave Wilma the nickname "Skeeter" because she was so tall and thin. Her long arms and legs made her look like a mosquito, and she had such high energy, she was always buzzing around—"always in my way," he joked.

Mae called Wilma "Skeeter Baby," and she took her under her wing. She noticed that Wilma was nervous about fitting in with the other girls. Wilma still cared so much about being accepted that she didn't like to win a race against a friend. When she did, she worried that the person wouldn't like her anymore.

Mae knew Wilma's attitude had to change. She didn't come right out and tell Wilma to stop worrying about what people think. She didn't even tell her to compete harder. Instead she said, "Skeeter Baby, you really have the ability to perform as an individual." Wilma didn't understand what Mae meant, but Mae didn't explain. She gave her comment time to sink in.

I know I can outrun Mae, Wilma thought. *She is quick, but she has to take two steps to my one.*

Wilma tried to push that thought out of her mind. *I don't want to beat Mae. If I do, she might not like me anymore. The other girls might resent me too. I'm just a high school girl; I shouldn't beat the college girls, much less overshadow a star.*

Wilma was scared. There were sixty girls competing to be on the Olympic team, and the others were all older and more experienced than she was. She decided to go look at the stadium. If she saw where she had to run, she thought it might make her feel more confident. But the stadium was enormous. She gazed at it and imagined all those seats filled with people looking at her. She felt worse than ever. Thinking about the race made Wilma sick. She was nauseated and couldn't eat.

Mae came to her rescue. "Skeeter Baby, you want to make the United States Olympic Team?"

"I sure do."

"All right, all you have to do is stick with me in the race. Don't think about anything else. Just stick with me, and you'll make the team."

The day of the trials, Wilma waited anxiously. When the starting gun went off, she flew down the track. She still was nervous about beating girls she knew, especially about beating the ones she really liked and respected. But in spite of those fears, Wilma had developed the concentration that all good runners must have. She was so focused on her own running that without knowing it, she passed Mae. Mae put on speed, and they finished at the same time.

When Wilma realized what had happened, she was horrified. Would Mae be mad at her? Would she lose her friendship? But Mae rushed over to Wilma, a big smile on her face.

"Skeeter Baby, you know what? I told you to stick with me; I didn't say beat me." Then she spoke seriously. "I'm going to retire, and you're ready to replace me. This race wasn't a true tie. You really beat me. Why did it take you so long to whip me?"

Wilma didn't know how to answer.

"We all knew you had it in you, but you wouldn't let it out. Today you did, and I'm glad." Mae was absolutely bubbling with happiness.

Wilma nodded. She was beginning to understand what Mae had so gently been trying to tell her. Now Mae spoke more directly. "Skeeter Baby, you have to always run your best. Run as an individual. That's how you help the team."

At last Wilma understood that a team player has to give her all, even if she beats her own team members. A team can't be strong otherwise. She never held back again. After that race with Mae she wasn't afraid to challenge anybody anywhere.

Wilma qualified for the 1956 United States Olympic Team. She would compete in Melbourne, Australia—a city and continent she had never heard of.

People back home in Clarksville, Tennessee, had heard of it, though, and they knew about the Olympics. They also knew that Wilma's family didn't have any extra money.

Mrs. Walter made Wilma two new dresses. Mrs. Simpson got her dress shoes to match. Her mother's Sunday School class collected money to pay for luggage. Her father's friends bought her running shoes.

"We don't need charity," Father protested.

"It's not charity," Mr. Thompson answered. "Wilma is representing Clarksville and the whole U.S.A. We want to be part of that."

"We are going to give her a party, too," Mrs. Thompson said. "She deserves a big send-off."

Wilma was grateful for the support of all their friends and neighbors. Everyone seemed to be taking care of her. Coach Temple got her passport for her. He said, "Wilma, you lose this little thing, you might never get back home. So I'm giving it to Mae for safekeeping."

They flew to Los Angeles for training. It was Wilma's first time to fly as well as her first Olympics, but it was Mae's third Olympics. "Skeeter Baby, it's great to win medals, but the important thing is the chance to travel and make friends with people from other countries. You just wait. You'll see what I mean."

The XVI Modern Olympiad

In 1956 in Melbourne at the XVI modern Olympiad, every girl had to be in by nine o'clock and no men were allowed to visit their rooms. Since the girls were focused on their events and didn't want to stay out late or socialize, they didn't mind. The rules were familiar to Wilma. What was different was that there were so many types of people—Asians, Mexicans, Africans, Scandinavians. There were people from all over the world, all with distinctive looks and accents, but all of them were serious athletes, and all of them had the same goal.

People from other countries were fascinated with America. It surprised Wilma that anyone would want her signature, but people did want it, partly because she was from America. That gave her an idea. She enlisted her American friends, and every day for at least an hour, they signed autographs. Wilma thought it was a friendly gesture that would be appreciated, and she was right. It also gave the American girls a boost to see that so many people were interested in them.

One of the athletes Wilma got to visit with was an Australian runner, Betty Cuthbert. Blue-eyed, blond, and wiry, she was the hometown favorite and the runner to beat. She was perky and had an open, friendly personality. As it happened, when Wilma met Betty, they chatted about shoes. Betty had wonderful, light running shoes made of kangaroo skin. They were so much better than what the

Americans had that Wilma felt a little resentment. It almost seemed that Betty had an unfair edge. Wilma didn't say that, but Betty picked up on her feeling, and she understood.

"Look," she said. "I know exactly where you can get shoes made for you just like this, right here in Melbourne. They cost between twenty and thirty dollars."

Wilma longed for a pair of those shoes, but she didn't have the money. Mae Faggs saw how badly Wilma wanted them. "Skeeter Baby, I'll let you have the money." Wilma looked down. Her father and mother would have to pay Mae back, and Wilma knew they couldn't afford to do that. She swallowed hard and shook her head. "No thanks."

Every day the American relay team practiced. They felt sure that they would be in the top three. They knew one another well, and if one of them lagged, the others would pounce on her and get her moving. Coach

Temple, their Tennessee State coach, wasn't there, though; he hadn't been selected as one of the U.S. coaches. That was a strong factor against them. They were getting sloppy about their baton passing. They were relying on pure speed, not skill.

If Coach Temple had been there, he would have scolded them in his quiet, firm way, and they would have paid attention. Even if he were there as only a spectator and even if they couldn't speak to him, his presence would have been reassuring. Something about Coach Temple made them feel secure. But he wasn't there, and they were on their own. That made things hard. Also, it was cold and rainy in Melbourne; the weather pulled them down. There was nothing to do but train, and training was not going well for the American runners. Their star long jumper, Margaret Matthews, fouled out of her event and did not qualify for the finals. It was not America's year; even Mae Faggs made it only to the semifinals. A lack of confidence pervaded the whole American team.

Wilma's first race was the trial heat in the 200. She blocked everything out of her mind except running and qualifying. She finished third, so she qualified. When they ran the semifinals, she finished third again, but the semifinals only took the top two. Wilma hadn't survived the trials; she lost her chance to compete in the 200.

"I've let down everybody back home. I've let down the whole U.S.A.," she said.

Wilma couldn't eat. She couldn't sleep. *I'm a failure*, she thought. *I'm a failure. I'm a failure.*

She closeted herself in her room. She didn't want to see anyone. But in the back of her mind was a very faint voice whispering, "Redeem yourself. Redeem yourself in the relay."

Wilma's thin, light body felt as heavy as lead. She could barely lift herself to leave the room. She had to force herself to go to the Olympic Stadium to watch her new friend

Australian Betty Cuthbert run. Betty won the 100, 200, and 400. She won three gold medals. That inspired Wilma. She spoke to herself as if she were her own coach. "You've got four years to get yourself to where Betty is now. Work hard for those four years. Pay the price."

She could start by making a good showing in the relay race. One of the runners had to be replaced because of a bad case of nerves. The team that finally represented the United States was an all-Tennessee State team made up of three veterans: Margaret Matthews, Isabelle Daniels, and Mae Faggs. The fourth member was Wilma. She was determined to do her best, although she suffered from her usual nervous stomach.

Mae Faggs was probably nervous too, but it didn't show. She seemed calm—as calm as a person can be who is building up a team's excitement. "Let's go get 'em. Let's give it all we've got. Let's make it into the top three and win ourselves a medal."

Mae's spirit was infectious. The other girls caught it. They were all eager to compete with the other five countries in the race.

Mae started the American relay. Her feet flew in those quick running steps that seemed so short to Wilma, and she approached the next runner, Margaret Matthews, without slowing down, and passed the baton. Margaret seized it without a pause, made her run, and passed the baton to Wilma, who ran like the wind in her long scissorlike stride. She passed the baton to Isabelle Daniels, who ran anchor like a true champion. She came in only two-tenths of a second behind the world-record-breaking Australian team anchored by the dazzling Betty Cuthbert, but they missed second place. Just the same, they had a strong, clean third-place finish.

When the four of them squeezed onto the victory stand to receive their bronze medals, Wilma's feelings were mixed. She wasn't happy about the 200, but she had to admit

that a bronze medal wasn't bad for a high school kid. Wilma also had to admit that Mae Faggs was right. The medal was only a part of the experience. The travel, the glamour, the excitement were just as important, and all the wonderful people were even more important. Betty Cuthbert was one of the most wonderful. Wilma cherished their frank, open friendship, as well as her new friendship with Bill Russell, the tall, black player who led the U.S. basketball team to an 8–0 record and the gold medal.

After the games the Olympic competitors didn't want to leave one another, but they had to, so they began to exchange gifts. They traded clothes—sweatshirts, shirts, uniforms. That was their way of giving one another other a small part of themselves. Wilma left carrying souvenirs and memories. And she carried a new goal. She would compete and win in the next Olympics.

Back to Normal

It was November, and in Clarksville, Tennessee, it was basketball season.

Coach Temple met Wilma at the plane. She was thrilled to see him. He told her that Burt High School had closed for the day, and that there was a special assembly for her. Everyone at the assembly cheered. People gave Wilma flowers. She even had to speak to the crowd that packed the auditorium. She told them that it was great to be back home. That was true. It was a wonderful day for Wilma Rudolph, but there was something weighing on her mind. As soon as she could leave the stage, she went looking for Coach Clinton Gray.

She found him. "Coach, this is Friday night, and I hear the first basketball game of the season is tonight. Is that right?"

"Yes, that's right."

"Look, Coach, I've been away at the Olympics and all, and I've been doing more running than playing, but I'll tell you something—I'm in great shape."

Coach Gray smiled.

Wilma took a deep breath. "Coach, can I play tonight? Please?"

Coach Gray laughed as he said, "Yes."

That game was the first in an incredible season. Burt High School had one of the best teams in the history of Tennessee. They won every game that season and were the first girls' team to score more than one hundred points a game. Wilma averaged thirty-five points a game and her friend Nancy

Bowen averaged thirty-eight. But things weren't always rosy.

"Hey, she's no better than we are. She ain't so hot."

Wilma overheard remarks like that during the basketball season. It seemed to her that after the Olympics, everyone expected her to be phenomenal all the time. Her friends acted differently too. She couldn't be just plain Wilma Rudolph anymore, except with Robert, who was now her boyfriend, and her best girlfriends, Nancy Bower and Delma Wilkerson. Other people either put her on a pedestal or knocked her down. Sometimes she felt like an outcast in spite of winning so many games, but the team made it to the state tournament again. It was in the gym at Tennessee State in Nashville.

Coach Gray was an emotional man, and on his teams there was always a mixture of love, friction, and conflict. He often lost his temper and shouted at his players. That showed he was really involved with them and with what they were doing, but it was unpleasant. He was especially emotional about this championship game because the Burt High team of Clarksville was playing against the Merry High team from Jackson. Coach Gray had gone to school at Merry High, so he had something to prove. He desperately wanted to win.

Wilma was not at her best. She had painful tonsillitis: She could hardly swallow, she could barely eat all week, and she couldn't say more than two words at a time.

Normally, when Wilma was open for a shot in the corner, she would yell for someone to throw her the ball. This time she couldn't yell. Instead she would clap her hands when she was open. But clapping was hard to hear over the cheering spectators, and the other players weren't used to it. They missed throwing to her several times when they should have. In the closing seconds of the game the Burt High team was ahead by only a couple of points. They were supposed to follow the standard last-second freeze— simply keep the other team from getting the ball and let the clock run out.

Wilma had the ball. Suddenly a player from Merry High stole it. The Merry team didn't make any more points, though, because the clock ran out before they could shoot.

The Burt team won the state championship. Their fans clapped and shouted for joy. They ran onto the court cheering and congratulating the players. Everyone was happy.

But Coach Gray screamed at Wilma. "Why did you throw the ball away like that? What a dumb thing to do! How could you be so stupid?!"

The cheering stopped.

The gym grew quiet.

Wilma snatched her jacket from the bench and ran into the locker room.

"What's wrong with that man?" she said

angrily to some other players. "Why'd he scream and yell at me like that? I hate him. He makes me sick. Why's he always trying to make an example out of me by picking on me all the time?"

Coach Gray was right behind the wall. He heard everything Wilma said.

When she saw him, he had tears in his eyes. He turned and quickly walked away. Wilma ran after him. "I'm sorry, Coach, but yelling at me in front of everybody made me feel awful."

She started to cry. The two of them stood together in the hallway, crying. Then they hugged and made up.

Coach Gray took the whole team out to dinner. It was a nice gesture, but there was tension in the air. Even though they were the champions, it didn't feel like much of a cele-bration.

A Night to Remember

Since Wilma had been old enough to date she had only gone out with one boy. It was Robert Eldridge, whom she had liked since she was six years old. Why bother with other boys since she liked him so much? He still had his lively personality and a funny, devilish streak. He was good-looking, too, and he was always neat, clean, and well dressed. He was the star of the school's football and basketball teams, and Wilma was the star of the girls' track and basketball teams. They were the most dazzling couple in school, and they were going to go to the junior-senior prom together. Wilma was sure it would be a night she would never forget.

Wilma's parents couldn't afford to buy her a dress, so she had to think of something. She remembered her elegant friend Shirley Crowder, and wrote to ask if she had a dress that would be suitable. Shirley wrote back that she had a beautiful blue evening dress that Wilma could borrow. She thought it would be perfect for her.

Wilma accepted gladly and waited in anticipation for the dress to arrive in the mail. At last a big box came. Wilma opened it, her heart beating fast. Inside was the most gorgeous dress she had ever seen. She hurried to put it on. It fit perfectly.

I look like a dream, she thought. *This is going to be the best night of my life.*

Robert borrowed something for the prom too—his father's brand-new blue Ford, and he bought Wilma a white orchid corsage. They arrived at the prom in high style.

Of course, no one was supposed to have liquor or tobacco at the prom, but the boys bought Thunderbird wine and sneaked it into the locker room. Girls shared cigarettes in the restroom. The windows were open, but when Wilma went in, the air was so thick with smoke she could hardly breathe. Just the same, she wanted to be part of things.

"Let me try a cigarette," she said.

A chorus of voices answered, "No! No! No!"

"Absolutely not," someone said.

"Coach Gray would kill us if we gave you a cigarette."

"Oh, come on," Wilma answered. "I deserve a little fun. It's prom night."

Finally they gave in. "Okay, take a puff."

Wilma didn't really know what to do with the cigarette. She put it in her mouth, breathed in, and choked. When she gave it back, the end was all wet. She had ruined it. Cigarettes were scarce, so Wilma's friends didn't give her a chance to ruin another one.

After the prom a lot of the kids decided to drive to Hopkinsville, Kentucky. It was about twenty-five miles from Clarksville. They knew of a nightclub there where they could be served drinks without being questioned about their age.

"Last one to Hopkinsville is a chicken!" they told one another.

They jumped in their cars and drove as fast as they could all the way. Wilma and Robert were the first ones there.

They had been there about an hour when they heard shouting from across the room. A bottle whizzed by Wilma's head. A chair sailed through the air. People swore loudly. Two men were fist fighting.

"Come on! Let's get out of here," Robert said. "This is no place for us."

He grabbed Wilma and headed for the door. Their friends, including Nancy Bower, followed. "Last one back to Clarksville is a chicken!" they told one another.

Robert and Wilma got a head start and arrived in Clarksville before the others. Wilma had arranged to stay with her friend Delma. Robert dropped her off, and she went inside and fell asleep.

At about four in the morning the phone rang. Wilma heard Delma's mother answer. "Why, yes, Coach Gray. Wilma and Delma are both here."

Wilma hurried to take the phone. Why was Coach Gray asking about her?

"Hello, Coach—"

"Oh, Wilma, thank God, thank God." He was crying hard.

"What's wrong, Coach? You sound terrible."

"Thank God, you're alive." He kept sobbing. At last he told her, "Nancy Bower is dead."

Wilma felt that she had been hit by a bolt of lightning. She went numb. She couldn't really believe what she was hearing. Later she learned that the boy who was driving the car Nancy was in had been drag racing on the way back from Kentucky. At ninety miles an hour, he lost control and crashed headfirst into a concrete pillar under a bridge. He and Nancy were killed instantly. The three passengers in the backseat were seriously injured and in the hospital.

Nancy had been Wilma's first friend outside of her family. Nancy was a great athlete; she always outscored Wilma in basketball. When other girls talked about clothes, makeup, and boys, Wilma and Nancy talked about basketball. They schemed together to find ways to play more often. Nancy always had more energy than she knew what to do with. She was lively and full of fun. Now, at sixteen, she was dead.

Wilma was devastated. It was a night she would never forget.

Yolanda

Except for her deep grief about Nancy, Wilma's life was bright. She looked forward to a great basketball and track season. She and Robert were seniors in high school. She wore Robert's football jacket, and he wasn't just the boy she liked anymore. She was in love with him.

When basketball season started, Wilma went to Dr. Coleman for her regular pre-season physical exam. "Wilma, I want you to come back in a couple of days. I want to talk to you privately."

She was surprised and wondered what he had to say to her. It was, "Wilma, you are pregnant."

She was too shocked to even answer. Pregnant? She could hardly believe it, but she knew that Dr. Coleman, who had seen her through so many illnesses and who had always been her understanding friend, was telling her the truth.

"You need to talk to your parents. You'll have a baby this summer."

Tell her parents? How could she do that? They would be crushed. She couldn't tell Coach Gray, either; telling would mean the end of her basketball career. So she kept quiet.

"What's wrong with you, Wilma?" Coach Gray asked. "You're getting lazy out there, not running after the ball, and you're getting kinda fat."

Wilma didn't answer Coach Gray, but he was determined to find answers. He went to see Dr. Coleman. "What's wrong with Wilma?"

Dr. Coleman didn't want to violate Wilma's privacy or break doctor-patient confidentiality, but he did want Wilma taken care of. He was worried that she might try to do too much and would hurt herself or the baby.

"Since you ask, I think Wilma may be working on a tumor in her stomach."

Coach Gray took a deep breath. Later he called Wilma to his office. "I saw Dr. Coleman, and I know he's covering for you. You're pregnant. This is serious. You need to talk to your parents."

Wilma nodded, but she was thinking, *I can't tell my parents. It would hurt my mother too much, and it might even kill my father. He is frail, and I'm the apple of his eye; he couldn't stand it.*

She didn't know which way to turn. Everything seemed hopeless. And Robert had started dating someone else. She felt that he was deserting her. Her world was falling to pieces. She had to tell someone. At last Wilma decided to tell her older sister Yvonne. It was hard, but she and Yvonne had confided in each other all their lives. It was easier to tell her than anyone else. When no one else was around, Wilma admitted that she was four or five months pregnant.

"Have you told Mother and Father?"

"No. I just can't. Mother has been giving me suspicious looks, though."

"Okay, Wilma. I'll tell Mother."

She did, and Mother told Father. The dark secret was out.

"I'll stick with you no matter what," Mother told Wilma. Wilma felt as if a crushing weight had been taken off her shoulders. However much she had hurt Mother, Mother still loved her and put Wilma's welfare first. Father was just as loyal. He blamed Robert, and he forbade Wilma to see him again, but he said, "Don't be ashamed. Everyone makes mistakes."

One day quite unexpectedly, Coach Temple appeared on the Rudolphs' doorstep. They invited him in, and he sat down with Wilma and her parents.

"I got some startling news," he said in his calm way. "I heard that Wilma is pregnant." Wilma nodded. Then she left the room. She was humiliated. She couldn't look Coach Temple in the eye. Why had he come? It was too horrible. She knew how he felt about girls getting pregnant. He had a standing rule that he would not take any girl who had a baby on to his track team. But, humiliated as she was, Wilma couldn't be rude to her gentle teacher—the coach who had taught her so much. She pulled herself together and went back to join him and her parents.

As soon as she came into the room, Coach Temple said softly, "Wilma, I still want you to come to Tennessee State after the baby is born."

Wilma was amazed. She was also thrilled

and grateful. Coach Temple was breaking one of his own strict rules for her. Her future as a runner wasn't gone after all.

But she couldn't run track for Burt High School. It should have been her best season, but her pregnancy was too advanced for her to run. She graduated, though, and in July 1958 Yolanda was born.

Keeping Yolanda

"That no-good Robert can't come in," Father told Wilma as she lay in the hospital bed.

Wilma was excited about her beautiful baby girl, but she longed to have Robert there admiring the baby with her. That was impossible. Father had not only told all the family to keep Robert out, he had laid down the law to the hospital staff, too. The staff did as Father said; Robert was barred. He couldn't even come in and peep at Yolanda through the glass.

Of course Robert couldn't enter the Rudolph home. He couldn't even be a part of paying his own baby's expenses. Father wouldn't allow it.

"Mr. Rudolph, I would like to pay half of Wilma's hospital bill," Robert's mother said.

Father shook has head firmly. He didn't want to be rude to Robert's mother, so he added, "No, thank you."

It was clear that even as poor as they were, Father wouldn't yield. He paid for everything himself. He put all the responsibility for the pregnancy on Robert, and he didn't want anything to do with him.

Delma Wilkerson came to see Wilma in the hospital. She carried a note from Robert. Wilma read it eagerly.

"I love you, and I want to marry you. We can have our own little place—just you, me, and our baby," he wrote.

Wilma talked to Father. "Robert wants to do right. He wants to marry me. He wants us to have our own place. His parents would help."

Wilma might as well have talked to a stone statue. Father would not be moved in his opinion.

The truth was that when it came to marriage, Father's unreasonableness was a relief to Wilma. Even though she loved Robert, she didn't want to become a housewife. Not yet. She wanted to go to college; she wanted to be a runner; she wanted to go to the Olympics in 1960. So Father wasn't the only reason Wilma didn't get married.

There was no way Wilma could study, run track, and take care of a baby, too. Mother had offered to take care of Yolanda for her, but Father got sick, and that changed everything. Now Mother had to work. She couldn't do that, care for Father, and take care of Yolanda. It was impossible.

They had to figure something out.

Wilma's sister Yvonne, who was married and had a five-year-old son, Tommy, came from St. Louis. Yvonne always came when

119

she thought she was needed. The three women put their heads together.

"Tommy will be in preschool this year," Yvonne observed. "I'll be free in the daytime."

"Do you mean you're willing to take care of Yolanda?" Wilma asked.

Yvonne looked thoughtful. "Maybe . . . I would . . . if I thought I could manage. . . ."

"I'll tell you what," Mother said. "If you'll take Yolanda, I'll keep Tommy. I can take him to nursery school on my way to work and pick him up when I'm through. That wouldn't be too hard. It's more convenient in this little town than it would be in St. Louis."

"Okay," Yvonne said. "I know I can take care of one baby. I've already done that. It's a deal . . . if it's all right with Wilma."

Wilma gave a whoop. "All right? I'll say it's all right!" She was going to college, going to run track, and her baby would be well cared for. She began getting her things ready.

One night only a few days before she left,

Wilma got up in the night to take care of Yolanda. She heard a rapping on the window. Frightened, she quickly turned off the light. She trembled as she stood in the dark. Was someone going to break in? Was someone going to hurt her? Perhaps someone wanted to snatch Yolanda.

The rapping came again.

Why would a person keep knocking if he's up to no good? she wondered. *Maybe someone wants to get my attention.*

Wilma took a few deep breaths. She got up enough courage to peep out the window.

There stood Robert, Yolanda's father!

Wilma knew that he had come to see his daughter. She knew he must be longing to hold his child and felt he should at least get to look at her.

Wilma opened the window, picked up the baby, and held her up. The baby girl's young father gazed at her through the screen. Wilma could see both happiness and sorrow

on his face. It was a brief but important join-
ing of their little family.

Yvonne took Yolanda to St. Louis; Tommy
came to Clarksville; and Wilma went off to
Tennessee State. She ran well and managed
to keep her grades up too. By Christmas she
was settled in and feeling comfortable, but
it had been four months since she had seen
her baby and her family. That was a long time
for her. Most students saw their families at
Christmas, but at Tennessee State, runners
didn't have Christmas vacation. The track
team had to stay at school and practice.

The team spent Christmas Eve in the dormitory and ran every day during Christmas
week. Coach Temple could see that morale
was low, so he decided to give the girls
three days off between Christmas and New
Year's.

Wilma wanted to see her baby, but three
days wasn't enough time to get back and

forth to St. Louis. She decided to talk to Coach Temple.

"Coach, could I have two more days off? My baby is five months old now, and I haven't seen her since September."

"Absolutely not! I'm going to treat you like everybody else—no special favors."

Wilma knew that Coach Temple had broken his rule against having a mother on the team just to accommodate her. She was lucky to be there at all. So she couldn't complain. She went home to Clarksville for the three-day break.

While she was there, Yvonne came from St. Louis. She didn't bring the baby; a friend was taking care of her. That was disappointing, and Wilma couldn't understand how Yvonne could come without Yolanda. She must know how Wilma longed to see her baby.

Yvonne took Wilma aside and spoke to her privately. "Wilma, I've become very attached to Yolanda. I want to talk to you about the possibility of adopting her. After all, you're in school, and I've got the time to take care of her."

"What?!"

Wilma couldn't say more than that. Her head was whirling. She had never thought that her sister would want to keep Yolanda. Yvonne had always been a good sister, but Wilma wasn't about to give her baby up. She felt that Yvonne was going to take Yolanda, that Yvonne was going to come between Wilma and her daughter and that she couldn't be her own baby's mother anymore. She was so frightened, she didn't even talk reasonably to Yvonne. Instead she spent the rest of the day in a frenzy.

How could she get Yolanda back? She wanted to go to St. Louis, but she didn't have any money, and she knew Father wouldn't give her any. She didn't have any time, either. Coach Temple was clear about that. But she had to do something. She went out searching for Robert. When she found him, she cried and told him her fears. He took her seriously. He knew how she felt, and what it felt like to lose a child. Together they worked out a plan.

"I'll get my father's car," he said. "And I'll take care of the money, too. But you have to deal with your father."

Wilma knew that part was up to her, and she knew it wouldn't be easy. She hurried home. "Father, I just have to see my baby. I can't stand it. Robert can take me to St. Louis."

Father was horrified. "What are you talking about? You can't go anywhere with that no-good Robert."

Wilma began to cry. "Father, it's the only way I can see Yolanda and get back to school on time. I'm dying to see her."

Father set his jaw. He wasn't about to change.

Wilma asked her brother Roosevelt to help. Once he agreed, Wilma went back to her father. "Roosevelt will come with us. He's a good chaperone. You can be sure I am safe when he's along. That way I can see Yolanda."

It took hours of crying and pleading—valuable hours out of three short days—but at last Father agreed to let Wilma go since Roosevelt would be along and had agreed to stay with them at all times.

Wilma went back and told Robert. Then they finished making their plan.

Neither of them wanted Roosevelt to go along. They decided to sneak away during the night when everyone was asleep—without Roosevelt.

At about three in the morning Wilma tiptoed out of the house, jumped into the car with Robert, and they were off. They drove all night, arrived in St. Louis, and went to Yvonne's house. They slipped in, snatched the baby, and dashed away. They headed straight back to Clarksville.

It seemed that they would accomplish their mission in record time, but the car broke down.

Robert called his father.

"Just wait right there," his father said. "I'll bring another car."

So Wilma and Robert had to sit at the side of the road almost all day. But at least they were together, and they had their baby to play with. Yolanda cooed and laughed. Wilma and Robert felt happy sitting there in the car with her, but they knew Wilma's father would be furious with them. Robert still couldn't enter their house, and Wilma couldn't expect a pleasant homecoming.

When they got there, Father was in a rage, but when he saw Yolanda, he calmed down. He took her in his arms, and she won his heart. It wasn't long until he said, "This baby ain't going nowhere. She's staying right here."

Wilma had to go, though. She barely made it back to Tennessee State on time. As for Yvonne, this was a rough time for the two sisters, but they had a strong bond and were able to overcome it.

Start Celebrating

Wilma was majoring in elementary education and minoring in psychology. When she got back to school, she had to work hard. It wasn't easy to keep her grades up since she had to put so much time and energy into running and into worrying about Yolanda. Although he didn't say so, she knew Robert wanted her to quit school and be a full-time wife and mother. Sometimes Wilma felt like doing just that. Sometimes everything seemed too hard, and she felt confused about what she should do.

"Would you please speak to me after class?"

Mr. Knight, Wilma's history teacher, said one day. That worried Wilma. Was something wrong with her work? Could she be doing badly in class? She worried all through the lecture. After class she went to Mr. Knight's desk and stood there shyly.

"Here, have a seat, Wilma," he said courteously. There was something reassuring in his manner. Wilma sat down. Everyone else was gone. The room was quiet.

"What's troubling you?" Mr. Knight asked. He seemed like a father or a kind uncle.

"Oh, Mr. Knight, it is such a fight to keep going. I just don't know what to do. I can barely keep my two-point grade average, and I'll lose my scholarship if I don't have the grades."

He nodded, encouraging her to say more. There was something comforting about him. He seemed to understand, so she went on.

"Running takes almost all of my energy and my concentration. That makes it hard to study, but that's not the main thing. . . ." She hesitated.

"Yes, Wilma. Go on."

"It's Robert—my baby's father. And it's the baby—my baby, Yolanda. I want to be a good mother, and Robert thinks I should quit school. He doesn't come right out and say that, but he keeps hinting. He says things that make me know how he feels and what he believes my duties are. Sometimes I think he is right. Besides, it is such a struggle. . . . I may give up and go back to Clarksville, but I can't get my thoughts straight. . . ."

That was a very long speech for Wilma. Mr. Knight had given her a chance to get things off her chest, and she had taken it.

"You have a lot to sort through," Mr. Knight said. "Maybe we can cut through the confusion if we think together." He began to ask her questions. Was Yolanda well cared for? Was she getting enough love and attention?

The answer to both questions was yes. The same people who had cared for Wilma were caring for Yolanda. They adored her, and her brothers and sisters who were near gave her loving attention too.

Did she really want to go back to Clarksville and be a housewife?

The answer to that was no. That life seemed too narrow for Wilma now, but she did want to be a good mother, and she did want to fulfill her obligations.

Did she think it would really be better for Yolanda if she gave up her college education? Would that actually be doing her duty?

Again the answer was no.

What about running? Would it be smart to throw away all those years of training and not even try for the Olympics? Would it be smart to toss away her future?

"Not smart," Wilma admitted. "Not smart at all."

"You can have it all," Mr. Knight told her.

"You can have family and career. Don't give up."

Wilma agreed. She would keep fighting.

Mr. Knight had been wonderful, and Wilma knew he was right. Just the same, she went back to her dormitory room, threw herself on the bed, and sobbed.

Amazingly, after Wilma had her baby, she became faster. Her speed was tremendous, and she looked forward to the Olympic trials. They were scheduled at the end of her sophomore year. Her running had improved and her style had changed. When she was fifteen and first began to train at Tennessee State, she ran straight up and down, clenching her fists and gritting her teeth. With Coach Temple's guidance, over time she developed a long scissoring stride that made sportswriters call her a gazelle, and she developed a relaxed looseness of muscles that made her seem to float along the track.

Coach Temple also taught her to lean toward the tape at the finish line in the famous "Tennessee lean."

It had been four years since she had run in Melbourne, and a lot had changed. The skinny high school girl had become a mother and a college student. One thing that hadn't changed was Wilma's will to run in the Olympics and win. To do that, she had to run in the National AAU meet and be selected for the Olympic trials. The meet was held in Corpus Christi, Texas.

While she was in Corpus, that old problem that she didn't know how to fight reared its ugly head again. All the competitors for the meet got on a city bus, but the bus driver wouldn't drive them.

"I'm not driving for niggers!"

"These are all members of the same team," someone explained, trying to speak calmly and politely.

The driver turned his back and walked

away. Another driver came, but he didn't seem happy about driving them either. It was a small incident, but bumping up against prejudice was always saddening to Wilma. It affected her attitude toward the race. Wilma's friend Vivian Brown, who always made Wilma run hard to beat her, wasn't enthusiastic either.

"I don't feel it in my bones today," she told Wilma.

"Me neither," Wilma answered. "I don't even want to run."

"Well, we don't have a choice; we have to give it a shot."

"Yeah. Let's get it over with."

Wilma ran the 200-meter and won. She heard her time called. It was :22.9. She knew that was good and that she had made the Olympic team. Satisfied, she went and sat beside Coach Temple.

"Doin' all right, aren't you?" he said. Mild Coach Temple had a twinkle in his eye.

Wilma nodded matter-of-factly.

One of the team members came running over. "Why are you sitting there? Why aren't you celebrating?"

"Gee, it's nice that I made the team," Wilma answered, "but I made it once before, you know."

"That's not what I mean. You set a world record!"

"I did?"

"Yes, you did. Didn't anybody tell you?"

Wilma shook her head.

"Well, then, I'm telling you. You just ran the fastest two hundred meters ever run by a woman!"

Wilma's face broke into a smile. "Let's start celebrating."

Wilma had set a world record, but the people in charge of validating there records took a year to make it official. Because of that, her achievment doesn't always appear in record books.

Rome

Wilma qualified for the 1960 Olympic team in three events—the 100, the 200, and the relay. She was happy about that, but she was even happier when she learned that Coach Ed Temple, who she said "stuck with me through thick and thin," was going to be the coach of the U.S. Olympic Team.

The team trained for three weeks at Kansas State University in Emporia, and they loved it. One of the coaches had a cabin on a lake, and they would go there after practice to swim and eat the big grilled steaks he cooked for them.

They had fun, but they trained hard, too. They ran three times a day. The practice sessions were harder than they had been in 1956. The girls were so busy that they didn't really get acquainted until the day they weighed in. Wilma weighed 129. Her weight at that height was supposed to be 140. After a week Coach Temple cut Wilma's practice sessions down to two a day, and after two weeks, he cut it down to one. He didn't want her to burn herself out before the big competition in Rome.

There were bicycles all over the Kansas State campus for the girls to use, but Coach Temple said firmly, "No bike riding at any time." He didn't want them to use their running muscles on anything except running. But when the practices were cut back, the girls felt bored.

"Those bikes are just inviting us to ride them," Wilma said.

So the runners jumped on the bicycles, took off . . . and got lost in the woods. It took a couple of hours for them to find their way back to campus. They were worn out, and Coach Temple was furious. He made them do extra running as punishment. The next morning they were so sore they had to help one another out of bed.

Wilma heard rumors about the runners they would be competing against. Betty Cuthbert, the amazing Australian runner, was going to be back for a last try even though people said she was too old. A beautiful blond girl from Germany, Jutta Heine, was winning all over Europe. She was as tall as Wilma, and that made Wilma uneasy. Then she told herself, *Wait a minute. What am I doing worrying about her? She should be worrying about me. I'm the one who set a world record. Who's she, anyway?*

Wilma was ready for the Olympics both physically and mentally. Having Coach Temple along made her feel secure and confident—so confident that she hoped to win three gold medals in Rome.

Rome seemed like a storybook city. Wilma saw the Colosseum, the catacombs, the Vatican. It was like seeing beautiful pictures from a travel book come to life. She liked it better than Melbourne, where the 1956 Olympics had been held. The Italians loved talking and laughing with the athletes. That made being there fun. Of course, the language was a problem, but the U.S. Olympic Committee gave the American athletes little Italian-English dictionaries. The athletes walked around town with them, and pointed to the words they needed. Finally they learned to say some of the phrases themselves. Wilma could see that the Italian people got a kick out of their efforts.

The Americans were in demand with the other athletes, too, who wanted to learn American dance steps. Wilma and the other American girls taught them steps they had learned from the television program *American Bandstand*. The athletes

from other countries were impressed.

"They think we are the coolest cats!" Wilma exclaimed.

Her workouts were going great. It was hot—one hundred degrees—but that was perfect for Wilma. She was used to running in the Tennessee heat.

One day Coach Temple called Wilma over to him. "You have a good chance to win three gold medals. I believe it so strongly, I've actually been dreaming about it. Three nights in a row, I dreamed that you won all three gold and were the first American woman to do that. I want you to make that dream come true."

"I will," Wilma told him.

But one day a track newsletter was circulating among the athletes. It listed the fastest times run by all the women in the Olympics. Wilma's name was there . . . on the sixth page. She was shocked and disappointed.

"The sixth page! And what about the world record I just set?"

"Don't worry about it. That newsletter doesn't mean beans; whoever put it together doesn't know anything. Nobody else can come close to you," Coach Temple told her.

Wilma calmed down. Another coach wouldn't have been able to make her see things clearly or boost her spirits the way Coach Temple did. He always knew what to say to Wilma.

The day before the first race in Rome, the girls went to a big green field behind the Olympic stadium. It was hot, and the sprinklers were on. The girls started running through the sprinklers. It was great fun, and the sun made little rainbows as they jumped through the spray and got soaking wet. Wilma decided to take one last jump before they quit. She leaped over a sprinkler and landed with one foot in a hole. Her ankle popped.

Wilma started crying. The ankle hurt badly. She was afraid she had broken it and that all her work was wasted. The girls carried Wilma to the trainer. He took a look at the swollen, discolored ankle, then made a horrible face that scared Wilma even more. But when he examined the ankle, he found that it wasn't broken. He packed it in ice and had Wilma carried back to her room. There, he taped her ankle tightly and elevated her leg. She had to stay in that position all night. She lay awake. Her first big Olympic race was scheduled for the next afternoon.

Wilma had trained hard. Years of work had gone into getting ready to race in the Olympics. Now she worried that she was about to lose all she had worked for because she had played in the water like a child.

How could I have been so silly? What was wrong with me? Can't I ever use my head? She felt she had messed up her career as a track star and had let down all the people who had helped her. She couldn't bear to miss the race. A small flame of hope burned in her heart. I have to sleep, she told herself.

I have to rest so I can run tomorrow. She pushed worry aside and slept.

The next morning she put her weight on her ankle. It held.

It's only a sprain. I can handle a sprain. I don't have to run any curves today— just the straightaway in the 100. But Wilma's own words only carried her so far. Coach Temple's words meant more. He sat with her on the bus ride to the Olympic stadium, and he kept telling her that everything would be all right. When they got to the stadium, the girls were lined up in the order of their competitions, and then were taken through a tunnel into the stadium. Coach Temple wasn't allowed to go through the tunnel, so Wilma was left alone. But he had done his work. Wilma felt calm. She lay on a bench with her feet up on the wall, waiting for her name to be called. She looked around at the other runners and felt sure she could beat them, ankle sprained or not.

Vil-ma!

At least eighty thousand people jammed the stadium. As Wilma walked toward the track, they started cheering and chanting her name, "Vil-ma, Vil-ma." It was a glorious moment, but Wilma knew she had to block it from her mind. She had to concentrate.

She told herself, *If you start smiling and waving and listening to the cheering, you're going to forget all about the reason you're here. To win.*

These were trial heats. Their purpose was to whittle down the number of runners who would compete in the finals. Other runners were jumping around, running, and wasting energy. Wilma stayed around the starting block and waited for the race to begin. She won both the first and second heats easily. The next day she won the third trial heat as well, but that seemed trivial next to her showing in the fourth. She won it in eleven seconds. That was a new world record. But the International Olympic Committee disallowed it because the wind velocity at her back was more than 2.2 miles an hour.

Wilma was upset. So was Coach Temple. Wilma had to use her willpower and concentration to put that disappointment out of her mind. She couldn't let it interfere with the finals. She was determined to forget about it. The fans didn't forget though. When Wilma went off the field, the press was there, thrusting microphones into her face, and she found herself surrounded by people chanting, "Vil-ma! Vil-ma!"

For the final in the 100-meter race the top three contenders were Wilma, Dorothy Hyman from Great Britain, and Jutta Heine from Germany. Wilma was insecure about Jutta Heine, a tall blonde with a stride as long as Wilma's, who carried herself like a real runner.

The competitors were tense as they went through the tunnel that led to the stadium. Wilma knew it was often hard to be so close to the people she was running against right before the race, due to the conflict between the respect and friendly feeling of one champion for another and the spirit of intense competition that is needed to win. Wilma looked the other girls straight in the eye, but she didn't say anything. It seemed better not to try to get acquainted, and in any case she was sure they wouldn't understand her southern black English.

Wilma conserved her energy and concentrated deeply. Starts were always a problem for her, but this one wasn't bad. She came out third, and then she started building speed. When she crossed the 50-meter line, she knew she was in good shape. By the 70-meter line, she knew the race was hers. She won by six yards. Dorothy Hyman came in second. And Heine hadn't been the threat Wilma had expected.

Again Wilma set a world record, and again it was discounted. She was so disappointed that she cried. But she had won a gold medal easily.

When she returned to her room, it was full of flowers and telegrams. The ones that meant the most to her came from people back in Clarksville, Tennessee. She also appreciated the telegram from Betty Cuthbert, her friend the Australian runner, who had won three gold medals in 1956 and who had so inspired her. Betty had been injured and couldn't run anymore, but she was happy for Wilma. She was a good friend and a good sport.

In the 200-meter final Wilma would have to run curves, and she knew that might be a problem with her sprained ankle. But Wilma loved the 200 more than any other race. Sometimes she smiled to think how she had once told Coach Gray she hated the 200 so much she would never run it again. The day of that race was rainy and miserable; that added to her problems. Keeping up speed on a wet track was difficult, and with her sprained ankle, it would be easy to slip. She psyched herself up, saying, *There's nobody alive who can beat you in the 200. Go get it.*

She won the race against Jutta Heine and Dorothy Hyman, but the rain slowed her down. Her time was twenty-four seconds. She usually ran the 200 in :22.9. She was a little unhappy about her time, but it earned her a second gold medal. Rain drenched the stadium, but Wilma, wearing a floppy straw hat with a red and black band, went to the gate of the Olympic Village and signed autographs until six Tennessee State girls rescued her from the crowd and the rain. Wilma didn't care about the rain. Her mind was on her next event, the relay race. If she could only win the 4 x 100-meter relay, she would be the first American woman to win three Olympic gold medals.

Wilma's teammates for the relay were Martha Hudson, Barbara Jones, and Lucinda Williams, her friend and roommate. They had set a new world record in the semifinals when they ran against the Soviet Union, Poland, and Australia. Now, in the finals, they almost lost the victory. Lucinda Williams ran third leg and passed to Wilma. The baton bobbled, and Wilma had to stop to grasp it. Jutta Heine flew two strides ahead of her. Wilma put on a furious burst of speed, came from behind, and leaned into the tape to win the race and her third gold medal—all with a sprained ankle. Newspapers called her the "Black Gazelle" and the "Black Pearl."

The team set a world record too, and this time there was no question. It was officially awarded. It was a heady moment when Wilma stood on the victory stand to receive her third gold medal. After "The Star-Spangled Banner" played, she was swarmed by fans and reporters. People pounded her on the back, hugged her, and pushed microphones into her face. The crowd was so wild that the American officials finally grabbed her and escorted her to safety. One of them said, "Wilma, life will never be the same for you again."

Unfortunately, some of the changes were unpleasant. Wilma's youthful fear that people wouldn't like her if she beat them was realized. Her teammates were jealous and didn't like her anymore—all but Lucinda Williams, who remained a loyal friend. The atmosphere was sour, and Wilma longed to go home to Clarksville and be with family and friends.

American Olympic officials and Coach Temple had other ideas. They were eager to take advantage of the Olympic glory Wilma had brought to the United States, so they quickly arranged a tour. Wilma and the relay team, along with Earlene Brown, who had won a bronze medal in the shot put, were members of the touring group. They went to Frankfurt, Germany, where Wilma was given "the world's fastest bicycle for the world's fastest woman." They went to an invitational meet featuring Olympic winners in Stuttgart, Germany. In Athens, Greece, she competed in the stadium where the modern Olympic Games began. They also went to other meets, including one in Holland and the Empire Games in London where a life-size statue of Wilma was placed in Madame Tussaud's famous waxworks museum.

London was dark and dreary with rain and fog. On the London streets, you couldn't see ten feet in front of you, and Wilma imagined

Jack the Ripper at every corner. Although the weather and the attitude of her teammates made things gloomy, Wilma won her races. Winning all the time seemed to make the other girls angrier. Some of them were from Tennessee State and were girls Wilma had been living with and running with for years. It hurt to see that they had turned against her because she succeeded. Some of them stopped speaking to her.

In London the team was to attend a banquet one evening. It was an elegant affair, and they would all try to be graceful representatives of their country. Of course Wilma went running that afternoon, even though it was raining. Nothing could interfere with her staying in good form. When she returned to the hotel, she had about two hours to get ready. That should have been plenty of time. But someone had hidden the hair curlers. Wilma's hair was a mess from running in the rain. Frantic, she looked everywhere, but they were nowhere to be found. Finally she had to go to the banquet with her hair a mess. Dignified Coach Temple blew his top. When he questioned the team, they all played dumb.

The next day the team had to run the relay in the British Empire Games. The other girls decided they weren't going to try to win. They would just run fast enough to stay in the race. Incredible as it sounds, the team that had just won an Olympic gold medal and set a world record, decided not to make a good showing. White Stadium in London was packed with people who wanted to see the fastest women's relay team in history, but the team was going to let them down. It was another way of trying to embarrass Wilma.

The girls barely straggled along in the race. By the time Wilma got the baton, one girl on the opposing team was 40 yards ahead of her with only 110 yards to go. Wilma realized what her teammates had done, and she was determined to win. She wasn't going to let

155

the fans down, and she wasn't going to let her teammates succeed in their mean trick. She put all she had into her run. She ran the fastest anchor leg of her life, caught up with the opposing girl, and managed to win by a hair.

The crowd went crazy. Wilma got a standing ovation.

Naturally that amazing win didn't warm Wilma's teammates to her. Especially since Coach Temple saw through their scheme and said so. He was furious and told them when they got back to Tennessee State, they would be on probation. After that there was so much animosity in the air, life became almost unbearable. It was a relief when Coach Temple said they were going home.

Life at the Top

Wilma couldn't wait to get home. She wanted out of the poison atmosphere. She wanted to share her gold medals with the people who meant the most to her and who would be proud of her and appreciate that she had accomplished what she set out to do. She started the long journey eagerly. The team would return to Rome, fly from there to New York City, from there to Nashville, and then Wilma and Coach Temple would drive the fifty miles to Clarksville. That meant many days in airplanes and airports, but at least they were headed in the right direction.

When they finally arrived in Nashville, a huge crowd greeted Wilma. There were mayors of several cities, the governor of Tennessee, and marching bands, all there to greet her. That was gratifying, but Wilma just wanted to get home. Then Coach Temple dropped a bombshell. "You've got to stay here in Nashville for a couple of days."

Wilma couldn't believe it. "Why?"

"Because the people of Clarksville have a big celebration planned, and it's not ready. It is going to take them a couple of days to put things together."

Wilma felt terrible. She couldn't stand it. So that night she drove the fifty miles to Clarksville and snuck in to see her family. The next morning she was back at Tennessee State at wake-up time. As she put it, "That's running."

Wilma's Olympic achievement broke racial barriers. The big parade in her honor was the first integrated event in the history of Clarksville. It included the traditional all-white organizations and all the traditional all-black organizations. It began two miles outside town. Wilma rode in an open convertible and waved to everyone along the way. Her mother and father, her baby, Yolanda, and one of her brothers and his wife were in the motorcade. Former teachers and all the people who had been important in her life lined the streets—with the exception of Robert, the father of her child and the man she was still in love with. He had chosen to go to Indiana to visit relatives.

The banquet that night was at the Clarksville Armory. It was the first integrated banquet Clarksville had ever had. Judge Hudson, an old white judge, made a speech. He said, "Ladies and gentlemen, when you play a piano, you can play very nice music by playing only on the black keys, and you can play very nice music on the same piano by playing only on the white keys. But the best music comes out of that piano when you play both the black keys and the white keys together." Wilma felt that by winning three gold medals and being the cause of two integrated events, she had finally found a way to fight prejudice. That was a great victory.

In her own speech Wilma gave the pledge of a victor in true Olympic tradition. "I shall always use my physical talents to the glory of God, the best interests of my nation, and the honor of womanhood. I give you my humble thanks for the opportunity to serve."

There was terrible moment that evening: Wilma's father collapsed right on the stage. That was terribly frightening, but he recovered and refused to go home. "I'm all right. Just leave me alone." He didn't want to miss anything and stayed to the end.

Wilma didn't get to remain in Clarksville long. She had to participate in a homecoming celebration tour across the nation. She covered every state in the union, but the planned tour was interrupted and delayed when Wilma hurried home because of the death of her father. He had been a loving father—strict, difficult, and devoted. Wilma had adored him. She was deeply saddened by his death, but it comforted her that he had lived to see her as an Olympic champion. She knew that *her* triumph had been a triumph for *him*.

When Wilma resumed the tour, she met Roy Wilkins, Lena Horne, Harry Belafonte, Mayor Daley of Chicago, many senators, and many ambassadors, some of them from countries she had never heard of. When she was in Washington, D.C., along with Coach Temple and her mother, Robert Logan, an old friend from Tennessee State who had a job in the government, came to see them. "Don't run away," he said. "Hang loose. I'll be back to you."

Before long, he phoned. Coach Temple

answered. When he hung up, he said, "Get dressed; we've got a big surprise coming."

They were going to go to the White House and visit with President Kennedy.

"Why?"

"Because he invited us."

Robert Logan had told the president that Wilma was in town. They went to the Oval Office. Secret Service men were all around. They were cordial and chatted with them about sports. Soon President Kennedy came in, smiling his famous smile. He tried to put everyone at ease. "What's everybody doing standing around? Let's all have a seat."

He walked toward his rocking chair, paused, and started talking to Wilma about track. Then he sat down—and missed his chair. He fell smack on the floor. Everyone ran over to help him, all very serious, but President Kennedy was laughing. Everyone else started laughing too.

He chatted with Wilma for half an hour. "It

is really an honor to meet you and tell you what a magnificent runner you are," he told her. Then he visited with both her mother and Coach Temple.

That was Wilma's most memorable event of the tour. More important, however, was that she was able to continue fighting prejudice. She broke another barrier—this time the barrier against women. She was the first woman to be invited to run in meets that had traditionally been only for men. Those included the Los Angeles Invitational Indoor Track Meet, the Milrose Games, New York Athletic Club Games, the Penn Relays, and the Drake Relays. Wilma's participation helped open the doors of these events to women competitors.

In January 1961, when she was twenty-one, she was the star attraction at the *Los Angeles Times* Indoor Games. She ran the 60-yard dash in 6.9 seconds. That set a new world record. Vivian Brown ran second. Wilma encouraged her; she remembered Mae Faggs's encouragement, and she tried to give the same encouragement to Vivian. She set an example by repeating her victory in the 60-yard dash at the Milrose Games in New York City and by equaling her own world record.

At the New York Athletic Club Games on February 17, she beat her record by a fraction of a second. The next evening she was expected in Louisville, Kentucky, to open the first meet of the Mason Dixon Games. She had a painful bruise on her hip. Even worse, there was an airline strike, and direct flights to Louisville from New York weren't available. She flew to Atlanta and waited there in the airport for seven hours. At last she got a flight to Louisville. She arrived just forty-five minutes before she had to run. In spite of being tired and having a bruised hip, she set a new indoor world record of 7.8 seconds in the 70-yard dash. It was her second world record in twenty-four hours.

Wilma's life was not simple. She made hundreds of appearances, received two hundred letters a day and ten marriage proposals a week. She was still in school and was working at the school's post office. She had to keep up with her studies, work, and practice track.

In December 1960 European sportswriters voted her Sportswoman of the Year—a first for an American. In 1961 she was chosen Woman Athlete of the Year by the Associated Press. So many trips, speeches, and banquets on top of her already full schedule exhausted her. She collapsed at a national indoor meet in Columbus, Ohio. She lost the 200-yard dash to Vivian Brown by two-tenths of a second. It was the first time Wilma had lost a race in nearly two years.

Wilma felt that if she went back to the Olympics in 1964, she would have to win at least three, perhaps four, gold medals for her competition to be significant. She would have to compete with her own record. That wasn't appealing, so she decided to retire. Since no runner can go on forever, it seemed to her to be a wise choice to stop when she was at the top, even though she was young. Also, Wilma wanted to make changes in her personal life. Yolanda was still with Wilma's mother, and Wilma felt that it was time for her to assume care of her child. She watched for the right moment.

One day Coach Temple asked, "Rudolph, you up to competing against the Russians?"

"Why not?"

"There's a meet with the Soviet Union coming up at Stanford University in Palo Alto, California. You want me to enter you in it?"

"Yes, do. That's a good meet," she said, but she thought, *That's a good* last *meet.*

Wilma started working seriously, and Coach Temple pushed her hard. She suspected that he was rough on her because he knew she was considering marrying Robert. He didn't approve of that. All the hard work paid off, though; Wilma was in peak form.

The newspapers in Palo Alto, California, were full of stories about the wonderful Russian runners. Wilma didn't let that worry her, and she won the 100 easily, but she knew the Russians were best at the relay. In that race Wilma was given the anchor leg, and when she got the baton, a Russian girl was some forty yards ahead of her. Wilma tore out after her, picking up speed as she ran. The Russian looked at her out of the corner of her eye, a surprised expression on her face. Wilma caught up, passed her, and won the race. The crowd leaped to its feet in a standing ovation.

Time to retire with a sweet taste, Wilma thought.

After the event she sat under the stands and signed autographs for an hour. Then she went to a bench and started untying her track shoes. A little boy had been waiting, hoping to get an autograph, but he had been shoved out of the way by the older people. He shyly went over to Wilma, a pencil and a little piece of paper in his hand.

"Miss Rudolph, can I please have your autograph?"

"Son, I'll do better than that."

Wilma had a ballpoint pen, and she signed her name on both her shoes. Then she handed them to the little boy.

"Are you giving me your track shoes?" She nodded and smiled. She didn't hang up her track shoes, she gave them away. She was twenty-two years old.

Retirement

After she retired from track, Wilma made two goodwill trips. One was to Japan for the Baptist Christian Athletes. Reverend Billy Graham made the trip with that group. It was an honor to Wilma to travel with him since she was reared in a devout Baptist family. The other goodwill trip was to French West Africa for the United States government. Visiting Africa was a great experience for her. She was struck by the handsome beauty of the people, their flawless ebony skin, their excellent posture, and the grace of the women in their flowing dresses.

In Dakar, Senegal, Wilma was intrigued by the everyday life of the people. She even played hooky from a scheduled round of sightseeing in order to spend time quietly with the large family of her student guide. It was a pleasure to be taken into their home and to really get to know them. Soon she wore a flowing robe over her tennis shoes. She commented:

I really enjoyed Africa. There is something about the people that makes you fall in love with them. I just felt at home. They were very nice to me and I had a chance to be natural. I went everywhere. I even went to a place they called the "Medina;" it's a slum area. I just went out like I belonged there. They accepted me and that's what I wanted them to do. And whatever they wore, I wore. They wore short pants and tennis shoes; I wore short pants and tennis shoes. Sometimes they went without shoes; I went without mine. The women have a hairstyle. They wear a bandana around their heads, so I wore one around mine.

But most of the time Wilma was working. She had just had minor surgery before the trip, but she autographed a thousand photographs, made presentations on the radio, appeared on television, met the press everywhere, and gave out gold medals to the winners at the Friendship Stadium. She did it all with such grace that a French embassy official commented rather enviously that America had won more prestige from the small amount of money spent on Wilma's travel expenses than France had gained from the four million dollars it spent on the games.

As soon as Wilma got back to Clarksville, she went straight to Burt High School to see Coach Gray, just as she always did when she came back from a trip. She would often surprise him by putting her hands over his eyes and making him guess who it was. She and Coach Gray had had some difficult moments, but he was her first coach, and their bond was a strong and special one.

This time he wasn't in school. That was unheard of. He never took sick days. He was so dedicated, nothing ever kept him from school. Wilma decided to finish unpacking, then drive over to his house to see what was going on. Before she finished hanging up her clothes, Robert walked in. His face showed that something terrible had happened. "Coach Gray . . . he's been killed in an automobile accident."

Wilma rushed to the school in a daze and ran to Mrs. Mildred Jones's room. Mrs. Jones was Coach Gray's good friend. She would know the truth. When Wilma saw Mrs. Jones's face, no words were needed. The expression told her that Coach Gray was dead.

Wilma was shattered. She didn't see how she could make her scheduled trip to the

Orient. Mrs. Jones persuaded her that she should. "Coach Gray started you on your life as an athlete. He would want you to go; it would be a tribute to him." So Wilma wrote a letter to be read at his funeral, and went on the trip. The services would have been too much for her anyway. She preferred to think of Coach Gray as just being off on another job and to remember the good times.

When she returned from her two-month trip, the high school offered her Coach Gray's job as girls' track coach as well as a position teaching second grade in the elementary school she herself had attended. That was a compliment.

Also, she and Robert were ready to get married. No church in Clarksville was big enough to hold the crowd that would come to their wedding, so they used an open field. They set up an altar and had pale blue flowers and plenty of seats for all the guests. Robert and Wilma's families and friends surrounded them. Robert's sister, two of Wilma's sisters, and their six-year-old daughter, Yolanda, were in the wedding. Robert was so nervous he didn't even notice that his shirt had some buttons missing.

It was a festive event, but Coach Temple still didn't approve of her marrying Robert, and he didn't come. That hurt Wilma. The other sour note was that one of Robert's old girlfriends came and cried all during the ceremony. Moreover, a photographer from *Jet* magazine took the girl's picture, and it appeared in the next issue. Tears were running down her face, and the caption said, "Who was this woman crying at Wilma Rudolph's wedding?"

The happy couple had to settle for going to a reunion of Robert's family instead of going on a honeymoon. They didn't have the money for a trip, so they said they had seen so much of the world already they didn't need to go. Wilma got to meet all Robert's relatives at the reunion, and they prepared for their new life together. He enrolled in Tennessee State, and she started her teaching and coaching job.

Wilma loved teaching, but she had the whole job of supporting the family because Robert was in school and didn't make any money. She was frustrated by her low salary as a teacher, and by the stuffy atmosphere in Clarksville. She wanted to bring new ideas and methods into the school, but the people in charge wanted things to stay the same. She had barely finished the school year when, on May 19, 1964, her second daughter, Djuana, was born. Wilma watched the 1964 Olympics in bed with her new baby. She returned to teaching in the fall, despite her dissatisfaction, and the next August her first son was born. They named him Robert Jr., but when his father walked into the hospital room, he said, "Hey, I finally got a dude." So baby Robert was always called "Dude."

Wilma had a job offer to be the director of a community center in Evansville, Indiana. She decided that since she wasn't making money and wasn't able to make the innovative changes she wanted to as a teacher in Clarksville, she should take the position. She and her family moved to Indiana even though she knew the job was not what she wanted to do permanently. The problem was, she didn't know exactly what she *did* want to do. She only knew she wanted to be challenged and make a difference. She wrote to Berdetta Washington, a leader in the Job Corps, inquiring about a position. After an interview in Boston, she was offered a position at a Job Corps center in Poland Spring, Maine, running the girls' physical education program. She got to do everything—write the curriculum, conduct calisthenics, and organize the program. So away the family went to Maine. While she was there, she received a letter from Vice President Hubert

Humphrey asking her to work for him as a member of Operation Champion, a program that took star athletes into the sixteen largest city ghettos to give sports training to the young people who lived there.

Wilma jumped at the opportunity. She went to Detroit, Cleveland, Chicago, Washington, and other big cities. The conditions were terrible, and she could understand why the cities were exploding in riots—the oppression was so severe, the opportunities so few, and hope so limited. Nothing she had experienced in segregated, rural southern poverty had prepared her for city ghettos.

Next Wilma went back to Detroit to take care of her sister Charlene, who was sick. While there, she accepted a teaching position at Pelham Junior High. It was on Twelfth Street, the street of the famous Detroit riot. She believed that the kids there just needed outlets, and she gave them one through track. They loved it, and she loved working with them. Just the same, eight years had gone by since she won her three gold medals and she still hadn't found the fulfillment outside track that she had found in it. She resigned from Pelham after a year and a half, ever restless to find more for herself and her family.

On April 4, 1968, the same day that Dr. Martin Luther King Jr. was killed, her favorite aunt, Matilda Rudolph, died in Clarksville. Wilma flew to Nashville with her children. Tension filled the air on the plane. Everyone was thinking about the assassination of Dr. King, but nobody said a word. In Nashville, Wilma and her children had to catch a bus to Clarksville.

As she stood in the bus station, a white man came by and spat at her children. Wilma was ready to fight, but a black man who saw the whole thing intervened and called the police. They arrested the white man and took him away. Wilma had been fighting the good fight to help black people and to increase

179

understanding. Such persistent ignorance and hate was disheartening to her as she mourned the death of her aunt and the murder of a great leader. She became severely depressed. She had a long talk with Bill Russell, her friend from the 1956 Olympics who was now a big star with the Boston Celtics. She told him that she couldn't seem to pull herself out of her depression and that nothing in her life had gone right since the Olympics in 1960. She asked her friend for advice.

"Try something completely different, a change of scenery. Try California. If you don't like it, you can always come back."

Why not? she thought. She went to Los Angeles by herself and lived there alone for a while; then her family joined her. She worked for the Watts Community Action Committee, and she liked the work, but she needed more money. It seemed that she was right back at the starting line. How could she support her family on peanuts?

One day she got an invitation from the millionaire owner of an Italian newspaper to visit Italy for free; he said the Italian people remembered her and wanted to see her. It was a wonderful opportunity, and she jumped at it. When she arrived in Italy, a movie about the Olympics was being shot. Ryan O'Neal and Rafer Johnson were in it. She often went out with them. Wilma had fun in Rome; it was like a return to the past and was a temporary escape from her frustration about not finding a fulfilling career or making enough money in spite of having won Olympic honors. She hoped the trip would bring her peace of mind.

Then she caught cold and was sick in bed. One night while she was asleep, a young woman appeared in her bedroom. At first Wilma thought she was dreaming, but when she turned on the light, a pretty reporter was there. She asked Wilma a lot of questions.

"Look, I've got a cold; I'm confined to bed; this is the middle of the night; and you're invading my privacy. I'm not supposed to give interviews until they're cleared first."

The reporter left. The next day a big story about Wilma appeared in a Communist newspaper. It said that Wilma was being held prisoner, that she couldn't talk with anyone, that she didn't have a job and was living in poverty. It turned out that the newspaper publisher who had seemed so generous and sincere in giving her the trip was actually trying to exploit her for his own political ends. He was a Communist, and he wanted her to speak out against America and against capitalism.

Wilma called a press conference. "Look, I've got a cold; that woman appeared out of the blue in the middle of the night, asking questions. Who wouldn't be hostile? The story is true insofar as the job part is concerned, but the rest is false. I haven't found the work I want yet, but I'm not against America."

When she got back to the States, Wilma worked as a fund-raiser in Charleston, West

Virginia, where some people were trying to raise a million and a half dollars for a Track and Field Hall of Fame. She believed in the importance of the work. "Track is the one sport where American athletes get worldwide attention. Nobody in Europe knows American football players or baseball players, but they know the track stars."

When the million and a half dollars were finally raised, Wilma found that she herself was in debt, and Robert was very ill. They had to go home to Clarksville for a while. She and Robert had four children, but their marriage finally ended in divorce.

Wilma was determined to make her life count in other ways besides being a mother. She wanted to help young people, so she started the Wilma Rudolph Foundation in Indianapolis to help disadvantaged youngsters through sports and education. She told them, "The most important aspect is to be yourself and have confidence in yourself. And remember, triumph can't be had without a struggle."

The Wilma Rudolph Foundation is still in existence and works with thousands of young people every year. It teaches discipline, hard work, and dedication and is a living tribute to Wilma. It carries on her good fight. Her influence is also felt throughout women's athletics. When she stepped onto the track at the 1960 Rome Olympics, the performance of the "Black Gazelle" was viewed by a television audience of millions. Wilma inspired thousands of girls to join their local track clubs and to demand competitive opportunities in their schools. Her amazing talent captured the attention of the world media and thus promoted women's sports worldwide.

The "Black Pearl" was a symbol not only of grace, but also of achievement through hard work. She enhanced the image of black people and in so doing fought prejudice. Wilma Rudolph died of brain cancer at age 54 on November 12, 1994.